On the Flip Side

Also by Nikki Carter

Step To This
It Is What It Is
It's All Good
Cool Like That
Not a Good Look
All the Wrong Moves
Doing My Own Thing

Published by Kensington Publishing Corporation

On the Flip Side

A Fab Life Novel

NIKKI CARTER

Dafina KTeen Books
KENSINGTON PUBLISHING CORP.
http://www.kensingtonbooks.com

DAFINA KTEEN BOOKS are published by

Kensington Publishing Corp.
119 West 40th Street
New York, NY 10018

All Kensington titles, imprints, and distributed lines are available at special quantity discounts for bulk purchases for sales promotion, premiums, fund-raising, educational, or institutional use.

Special book excerpts or customized printings can also be created to fit specific needs. For details, write or phone the office of the Kensington Special Sales Manager: Attn.: Special Sales Department. Kensington Publishing Corp., 119 West 40th Street, New York, NY 10018. Phone: 1-800-221-2647.

KTeen Reg. U.S. Pat. & TM Off.
Sunburst logo Reg. U.S. Pat. & TM Off.

ISBN-13: 978-0-7582-7269-0
ISBN-10: 0-7582-7269-3

First Printing: March 2012
10 9 8 7 6 5 4 3 2 1

Printed in the United States of America

Acknowledgments

I have the most fun job in the world—writing books about drama! I love creating stories for my readers, so this time I'm thanking you first! Thank you for buying the books, for sending me Facebook inbox messages and posting stuff on my wall! I would love to see some of your reviews on Amazon.com. That would be so awesome . . . unless you hated the book. ☺ Just kidding! I want to hear it all! And I want to come to your school to talk about the sweet life of a young adult author. Get at me at authornikkicarter@gmail.com. (I do read these, by the way!)

My family is incredible. My husband and five children totally support me. Hello, Brent, Briana, Brittany, Brynn, Brooke, and Little Brent. Love you all!

My writer friends rock too! ReShonda, Eric, Rhonda, and Dee—thanks for the love!

And I have got the best besties on the planet. Shawana, Afrika, Tippy T., Robin, Brandi, Leah, Kym—love y'all bunches.

My editor, Mercedes Fernandez, is incredible. She pays me to say these things. ☺ For real, thank-yous go out to the entire team at Dafina and KTeen!

Above all, I thank God for the opportunities, talent, and tenacity to chase the dream!

Hope you enjoy!

Hollerations!

I'm on TWITTER! @_nikkicarter.

1

"Are you a free-thinking woman?"

I nod my head along with the other four hundred freshmen girls who will be my classmates at Spelman College. We're all seated in a huge auditorium, listening to the dean present our freshman orientation.

My roommate and new friend, Gia, whispers, "Can I be a free-thinking woman if I don't have boobs?"

"You think with your brain, not your boobs," I whisper back.

"Don't judge me until you've walked a mile in my padded bra," Gia says.

I cover my mouth to hush my giggle. I'm trying not to be noticed. It's hard enough being incognito as Sunday Tolliver, recording artist. Okay scratch that. It's dang near impossible.

Luckily Gia is not a starstruck groupie type. Not that I'm really a star yet, but it would be difficult if I was rooming with someone who wanted to know about my mentor, Grammy winner Mystique, or my cousin, Drama.

After the long speech by the dean we are dismissed for the rest of the afternoon to reflect on her words. Standing here in the courtyard, and gazing at our campus buildings, I feel inspired to learn, meet my new sisters, and change the world.

But first . . . lunch.

"Gia, do you want to go off campus to the Busy Bee Café?" I ask. "I'm starving."

"That's what I'm talking about!" Gia replies in the excited tone she uses with just about every sentence. "Let's do this!"

Even though I've only known her for two days, I like Gia so far. She's from Cleveland, Ohio, and just too excited to be in the ATL. I'm not mad at her, though. I never wanted to go to school anywhere else but Spelman.

"Wait a minute," Gia says. "Is the Busy Bee Café expensive? My funds are limited."

"It's not super cheap, but it's not expensive," I reply. I'm thinking she'll spend about fifteen bucks on a delicious soul-food lunch.

"Can I get something for ten dollars or less?"

"Not a whole meal with a drink, tax and tip. It's gonna be more like fifteen."

Gia shakes her head. "No can do. How about IHOP?"

I scrunch my nose and frown. "I do not like IHOP. I'll take you to Busy Bee, my treat. It'll be my welcome-to-Atlanta present."

Gia smashes her hand into her bony hip and pokes her

lips out. With her huge afro and cornrows in the front, she makes me think of one of those old Dolemite movies. All she needs is some bell-bottom pants and a halter top that shows her belly button. Oh, and some big gold hoop earrings.

"No, Sunday. You are not about to start doing that. I'm not gonna be taking money from you all the time because you're a pop star."

"One time is not all the time, Gia. Plus, I like sharing."

"Well, I guess. But just this time. Is it close enough to walk, or are we driving, since I'm lucky enough to have the only freshman on campus with a car as my roommate?"

This took some persuasion by my manager, Big D, and a donation to the music program by my mentor, Mystique. Neither of them feel comfortable with the idea of me walking the streets of Atlanta. They convinced the dean that I would only be safe if I had an automobile to drive where I needed to go off campus.

Whatever the reason, I'm glad to be driving, because when it comes to walking somewhere in this stifling August heat, I completely disagree.

"Did I hear someone say freshman and car in the same sentence?" A white girl with brown hair approaches and stops in front of me and Gia. She appraises us each with a simple head-to-toe sweep of her eyes. I guess she likes what she sees, because the smile on her face is genuine.

"Maybe you did . . ." Gia replies.

The girl sticks her hand out to Gia. "My name is Piper. This is my first time being in Atlanta, so I was hoping I could catch a ride with someone to get something to eat."

"I'm Gia, and this is my roommate, Sunday. I'm sure you're welcome to join us, right, Sunday?"

"Sure! The more the merrier."

"Well, can I bring my roommate too?" Piper asks. "She's just over there, talking to those girls in turquoise."

I nod. "Go ahead. We'll wait."

The girls in turquoise are upperclassmen members of Gamma Phi Gamma, one of the biggest sororities on campus. Piper's roommate seems comfortable talking to them, and looks a bit annoyed when Piper pulls her away. As they walk back toward us, all of the Gamma girls look in my direction and smile. It's weird. I know it's a Sunday Tolliver the Artist thing. But on campus, I'm just me. Sunday.

"Okay, calm down!" Piper's roommate fusses. "I said I'll go for crying out loud."

Between rapid breaths, Piper says, "This is my friend . . . Meagan."

"We're roommates," Meagan says with a little laugh. "I'm not sure we're friends yet."

Piper's face falls a little, and she seems to swallow all her bubbly excitement in one gulp. Then, Meagan gives Piper a little slap on the arm.

"I'm kidding!" Meagan says. "This girl is *super* sensitive."

Gia lifts an eyebrow and slowly extends her hand. "I'm Gia Stokes, and this is Sunday Tolliver."

"Meagan Morgan, of the D.C. Morgans," Meagan says.

Gia looks at me and I shrug. "I'm afraid I've never heard of the D.C. Morgans," I reply, "but I'm happy to meet you anyway."

"You never know who knows who at Spelman," Meagan says. "I'm just putting it out there in case we summered together when we were little."

Summered together? Where they do that at?

"Come on, y'all. My car is parked a little ways away. They let me have the car on campus, but not without making it real inconvenient."

Gia replies, "You ain't said nothing but a word, Miss Day-After-Saturday. I'm hungry den a mug."

Meagan furrows her eyebrows. "Translator!" she says with a giggle.

"Ahem . . . she said, 'That's the simplest thing ever, Sunday. I'm so hungry I could eat a cow,'" Piper says.

Gia frowns for a second while there's a moment of silence. Then, we all burst into laughter! Talk about breaking the ice.

"I do have, in my repertoire, an above-rudimentary grasp of the English language," Gia says. "But I reserve the right to take it skrait to da hood, baby! Ya heard?"

Piper high-fives Gia. "I know that's right!"

We cross the huge courtyard to the paid parking lots where my car is parked. I don't know how I feel about Piper cosigning with Gia and her hood-speak. Even though I used to have a white best friend, it just seems like Piper is trying a little too hard. I know we're at a historically black university, but really?

I hit the keyless entry on my Camry and Meagan stops in her tracks.

"This is what you drive?" she asks.

"Yes. Is there something wrong with my car?"

"No. Not really. I just expected you to have something a little more fabulous. You did hit number one on the *Billboard* chart, right?" Meagan asks.

I nod as I bite my bottom lip and get into the front seat of the car. "Are y'all coming?" I ask.

Is this how it's always going to be from here on out? Are people going to think things about me based on a hit record or a video? I had hoped that I wouldn't have this problem at school. My record *Can U See Me* was a hit, but now I've got to follow up with something just as good, maybe even better. It's enough stress trying to figure out how to have a great follow-up without worrying if the girls I meet here are going to like me whether I hit number one again or not.

Meagan beats Gia to the front passenger seat. I wish she hadn't.

"You know I'm kidding, right?" Meagan says. "Your car is great! The rest of us are hoofing it."

"Yes, you are," I reply as I pull out of my parking spot. "Put on your seat belt. I don't want a ticket."

"So," Piper says as I drive off-campus, "I know that Meagan is from Washington, D.C. Are you both from Atlanta?"

I open my mouth, but Gia already replies.

"I'm from Cleveland, Ohio," Gia says. "A place where it gets really, really cold in the wintertime, and doesn't get too hot in the summer."

"Well, I grew up all over the place," Piper replies. "But I spent my high school years in Jacksonville, Florida."

"You were a military brat, then?" Meagan asks.

"No. I was a foster kid. My last family that I had through high school was in Jacksonville. I stayed with a couple of relatives in Virginia and Alabama too, but I ended up in Jacksonville after I ran away from one of my aunts' houses."

"How in the world did you end up at Spelman?" Meagan asks. It sounds kind of rude, but it's exactly what I'm thinking, so I can't be mad at her.

"My foster mom went here, and I guess she's friends with one of the board members or something, because they got me a scholarship."

"Oh, you're on scholarship," Meagan says.

I hear Gia smacking her lips and sucking her teeth. One glance in the rearview shows the face I thought she'd be making. Lips poked out and eyebrows scrunched together.

"What's wrong with being on scholarship?" Gia asks. "Some of us don't have a city before our last name."

Meagan giggles. "Oh goodness! I didn't say anything was wrong with it. I was just putting two and two together. Like why a white girl would choose Spelman that's like ninety-nine-point-nine percent black when she could choose another school."

"I could've gotten a scholarship somewhere else," Piper says. "I had a four-point-four GPA in high school. I chose Spelman because I wanted to come here."

I pull into Busy Bee's parking lot. "We're here, y'all. Atlanta soul food cuisine at its finest."

A wave of sadness pours over me as we walk into the restaurant. My boyfriend, Sam, and I eat here a lot. Or we used to when he still lived in Atlanta. Now, he's at Fordham University in New York City, and I miss him so much. We went through so much drama to finally be together, and now we're separated. He promises that he'll be home all the time and that he'll call, text, and email me so much that I won't have a chance to miss him too much.

We go through the cafeteria-style line and order our food before taking a seat at a table. Meagan immediately unfolds two paper napkins and places them in her lap. She smoothes them out and then daintily places her hands in her lap.

Gia, Piper, and I stare first and then follow suit. It doesn't hurt anything to have table manners, and Meagan looks pleased.

"So," Meagan says, "let's go around the table and give the vitals. We already know where each of us is from, so let's find out the other important things: Do you have a boyfriend? Which sorority will you pledge? What's your major?"

When none of us speak, Meagan continues. "I'll go first. I do not have a boyfriend yet, but I will find one this year at Morehouse. I will pledge Gamma Phi Gamma. My mother was a Gamma and so was my grandmother. My major is communications with a minor in journalism. I will be a news anchor in Washington, D.C., when I graduate."

Gia looks at me with her jaw hanging open. I totally feel the way Gia looks. Who has it together like that?

"I do have a boyfriend. His name is Sam," I say. "I don't know about being in a sorority. I'm not sure if I'm the type, and I'm majoring in pre-law. I want to be an entertainment lawyer."

Piper's eyes widen with an expression of shock. "You want to be a lawyer? But you're a pop star! You make millions, right? Why wouldn't you just want to travel and have fun?"

"I haven't made millions yet. Plus, I want to have a backup plan to my music career. What about you, Piper? What are your vitals?"

"I don't have a boyfriend, but I hope to meet one too! I also want to be in Gamma Phi Gamma, and I'm majoring in computer science."

Meagan chuckles and looks into her lap.

"Did I say something funny?" Piper asks.

"Well, it was funny, but not ha-ha funny. It was kind of like when you say 'that's funny' when you think something is strange."

Gia says, "Interpret please."

"Well, it's strange that she wants to be a Gamma girl. She seems more like a Beta Kappa Epsilon."

"I don't get what you mean," Piper says. "My foster mother is a Gamma girl."

"Yes, but Gamma Phi Gamma is super exclusive. If you don't come from money or have a founding family member, it's really hard to get in. I just don't want you to be disappointed. Beta Kappa is a lot more open to diversity."

Piper turns a deep scarlet shade of red. I'm glad that our food gets to the table, because it distracts a bit from the uncomfortable silence. Meagan really is off the chain, but she's right about Gamma Phi Gamma. They probably wouldn't take Piper off the foster-kid status alone. Plus, I've never seen a Gamma girl with a tattoo like the one Piper has on her shoulder.

Meagan stares at Gia's plate. She has smothered chicken,

collard greens, candied yams, and macaroni and cheese, with a big hunk of pound cake for dessert. Meagan only has baked chicken and salad.

"Are you really going to eat all that, Gia?"

Gia laughs out loud. "Yes, I most certainly am, future Gamma girl. I'm trying to get some curvaceousness jumping off, and I certainly can't do it with salad. Unfortunately, it is very hard for me to gain weight."

"Ummm . . . that is quite fortunate," Piper says. "I look at food and gain weight. Give us your stats."

"Okay. Yes, I have a boyfriend. His name is Ricky and he goes to Georgia State University on a football scholarship. He's also one third of my bestie triangle. The other two points are my cousin Hope, who also goes to Georgia State, and my other bestie, Kevin, who is a Morehouse man. No thank you to the sororities. Not my style. And I'm also majoring in computer science with a minor in mathematics."

"All of your best friends came to Atlanta?" I ask. "Y'all must be one tight clique."

"We've been friends since we were little. We all go to the same church back home. My uncle is the pastor. So yeah, we are super tight, but we didn't all plan to come to Atlanta. Kevin was actually trying to go to an Ivy League school, but the money wasn't quite right. He's going to be a doctor."

"Well," I say, "I don't have any sisters, or any really close friends from high school. There's one girl, Bethany, but we've been through so much that she and I have drifted apart. And then there's my cousin. . . ."

"Drama!" Piper and Gia say in unison.

"Right. Y'all know all about her, I guess, from the reality show."

Piper nods. "Yes! That show was off the chain. I loved the Truth-Sunday-Drama love triangle! And when Sam went ballistic on Truth and fought him at the club, and it was on YouTube!"

Meagan gives Piper a disgusted look. "You sound like a total fangirl."

"I am a fan. I love Sunday's music! Don't y'all?"

Gia nods. "I do. You are a great singer."

"Thank you," I reply. "But for the record there was never a Truth-Sunday-Drama love triangle. Truth and I were never an item. That was a straight fabrication."

Piper and Meagan exchange skeptical glances. Whatever! I don't have anything to prove to these girls. Gia is busy chowing down, so I'm not exactly sure what her thoughts are on the subject.

"Are you going to put out an entire album soon?" Piper asks.

"Soon. We're releasing another single first, and then I'll go into the studio to record the album."

"How are you going to do all of that and go to school too?" Gia asks.

"It's gonna be hard, but I'll have to juggle it. I think I can do it."

I take a bite of my fried chicken and chew it for a long time before I can swallow. The truth is I'm nervous about trying to have a recording career and go to college full time. I have no idea whether I can do it or not. I've convinced everyone: my mom, Mystique, Big D, and Epsilon Records that I'm going to be a success at being a free-thinking Spelman woman and a pop star.

But deep down, I'm a little scared. What if I fail?

I guess now, it's time for me to believe my own hype.

2

"So, since the album is already gold and heading toward platinum, I think your next single should be a big ballad," Mystique says as she, Big D, and I chill in her fiancé Zac's studio.

"I agree," I reply. "I think it should be 'The Highlight.'"

"Hmm . . . let me hear you sing a piece of it so I can think of a concept for the video," Mystique says.

I open up my mouth and belt it out a cappella. *"I don't know a lot of things/ And I haven't been around a long time/But I don't have to know it all/To tell you what's been on my mind/You are . . . so amazing/And if it weren't for you, and everything you do/I wouldn't be this happy/Loving you is the highlight of my life!*

"On that little bridge part you can do a run like this."

Mystique does some vocal acrobatics on the word *amazing* that are . . . well . . . amazing! I laugh out loud, because my voice is good, but Mystique's is incredible. I won't even attempt to copy that.

"So you like it?" I ask.

"Oh, yes! I love it. You and Sam are so gifted when it comes to songwriting. I knew that from the jump."

Big D says, "Every song on this record is hot. This album is gonna remind people of when Lauryn Hill first came out and dominated the charts."

"Don't go there, Big D," I say. "I don't even like to hear you say that out loud. I can't even touch Lauryn as an artist or songwriter."

Mystique says, "Sunday, you have the potential to surpass that. You don't understand how gifted you are. D, when is she gonna get it?"

He shrugs. "I don't know, but I wish she'd hurry up so we can get this paper."

I hear what they're saying and I want to believe it, but it almost feels like I'm being disrespectful to those who came before me. I don't ever want to do that. What I do want is to make my own history, for real, for real.

"So we're going to do a video for this song," Mystique says. "But since you're in school, it won't be a fabulous island thing. We can do it here!"

"That's hot!"

Mystique's fiancé, Zac, is none other than platinum-selling rapper Zillionaire. My cousin, Dreya, is gonna trip when she hears that my video is being shot in his mansion. She's gonna trip when she hears my song, because it's not her song. She pretty much stays in trip-out mode, so you know, it'll be pretty normal for her.

"Are you going to have time to put in any work on

Drama's album?" Big D asks as if he could read my thoughts. Did I conjure Dreya up?

"I've already done four songs for her, but she said she wasn't feeling any of them. I don't know if she wants me working on her next record."

"She should, because Epsilon Records is about ready to dump her for all those shenanigans between her and Truth." Mystique punctuates her words with all of the disgust I believe she feels for Dreya.

I get a sour taste in my mouth when I think about Truth—the rapper that helped start both me and my cousin's careers. He and Dreya have been on-again, off-again since we were seniors in high school, and the off-agains always had to do with him trying to holla at another girl (sometimes me) or putting his hands on Dreya.

They've been off since Dreya was mysteriously jumped by a group of girls, for no reason whatsoever. That's the cover story she's telling us. I think that Truth decided to use her as a punching bag for the umpteenth time, because he was salty about getting dropped from his record deal with Epsilon Records.

"Epsilon won't drop her until they see the sales of her sophomore release. They'd be crazy to do it before."

Mystique nods. "You're probably right. But her first record's sales weren't incredible. As a matter of fact, I think without the reality show and Sunday's songs, she would already be out of the conversation."

"I'll talk to Dreya and see what she wants from me," I say. "Maybe Sam and I can work on something over the holidays."

Big D shakes his head and frowns. "No can do. You will be doing promotional stuff for your record, since you can't do shows right now."

"You're hot right now, Sunday. Let too many months go by and you won't be," Mystique says.

"Aaargh!" I don't want to talk about boring industry stuff anymore tonight. I'm ready to go back to campus and crash with my newfound homies. "Can I go now? I've got homework."

"Yes, but please know that I need you at six p.m. sharp on Friday. We are going to walk through the video, and record it on Saturday. I'll have wardrobe and choreographers here."

"Why do we need choreography?" I whine. "This is a slow song."

"Because I think we're going to have you dancing part of it like a ballerina practicing."

I give Mystique my blank-eyed stare. I don't know the first thing about ballet dancing, and I know I probably can't pull it off.

"Oh," Mystique says. "We'll also have some hot models to audition to be your leading man."

Although Mystique seems to be thrilled by the option of a really cute boy, I really couldn't care less. Sam played my love interest in my last video, and he was perfect. I wish he could be in every one of my videos.

"Okay, Mystique and Big D. I'm going back on campus now. Don't get mad if I don't answer your texts right away. Y'all know I go to class, right?"

"That's what you're telling your mother anyway," Big D says.

"Why would I be lying to her? I'm the one paying for this!"

Mystique laughs out loud and gives me a high-five. "That's right, girl. You better be a boss!"

I hug Mystique and Big D good-bye. I'm so excited to finally have a chance to talk to Sam that I jog across Zillionaire's ceramic-tiled floor and throw open one of the humongous glass and iron mansion doors. I don't even make it to my car before I snatch out my cell phone to call Sam. Sweet! I have three missed calls. That means my sweetie misses me.

I press send to automatically call his number since he was the last to call me. He answers on the first ring.

"It's about time you broke away from your new boyfriend to call me back," Sam says.

"Funny! I was meeting with Mystique and Big D," I say as I get into my car. I can't help but smile at the sound of his voice. It seems like I haven't heard it in forever.

"Everything going good so far? Your roommate sounds cool from your texts."

"Yes! Gia is really nice. I like her a lot. I met two other girls, Meagan and Piper. The jury is still out on both of them though."

Sam laughs that husky, delicious-sounding laugh. "Why is the jury out?"

"Meagan is the rich, summers-in-the-Hamptons type, and Piper is . . . well . . . she's cool, but she reminds me of Bethany."

"She's white?"

"Yeah . . ."

"So, you gonna hold Bethany's craziness against every white girl that tries to be your friend?"

I guess it does sound kind of silly now that I have it repeated back to me. "No. She's cool. We're all in the same dorm."

"My roommate is really smart. He was some kind of prodigy at his school or something. He said he'd help me with my homework and exams and stuff, if I'd let him hang out with me."

I laugh out loud as I step into my car. "That's funny!"

"Naw, that's fortunate!"

Hearing Sam's voice on the phone makes me miss him more. "When are you coming home for a visit?"

"I just left Atlanta three weeks ago."

"Wow."

"But of course, I wish I was there with you." Immediately, he's apologetic. I ice him with silence as I pull away from Zac's mansion and drive down the street.

"It's cool. I'm doing a video shoot this weekend, and Mystique has promised that there would be lots of hot boys there to keep me company. So you don't have to wish anything."

"Dang, why it gotta be all like that?"

"Humph."

"You might as well stop, Sunday. You ain't about to play me, and you know it. I have you on lock."

I absolutely don't give him satisfaction that would come from me agreeing with him, but what he says is completely and totally true. He's got me on lock—and there's no one else I'd give the key to my heart.

3

When I walk back into my dorm, Gia has clothes strewn across both our beds. All types of eclectic, bright-colored pieces that I would never wear, shoes and handbags to match. She's standing there, with her long legs in tiny shorts and with her afro somehow expanded into big crinkled sections, held back with a headband.

"How'd you do that to your hair?"

"Oh, that's nothing. It's a braidout. Gel, water, oil, braids. Plah-dow! Twist out."

"It's pretty."

"Thank you. We're invited to a party, so you might as well pick something out."

"It's Wednesday. We have class tomorrow."

Gia drops the yellow Tweety T-shirt, on which Tweety has bedazzled rhinestone eyes, onto the bed in front of her.

"You're not going to be that roommate are you? For

real? We're in Atlanta, Sunday! And we don't have to stay out all night."

"I grew up in Atlanta! A party doesn't even sound that enticing to me right now. I'd much rather be going to bed."

Gia slides across the floor in her Tweety slippers (something about this chick and Tweety) and grabs me by both arms. "You have to go, Sunday! I don't want to walk up in there alone."

"What about your trio of besties? Your boyfriend? Why can't any of them go with you?"

"They can, but they can't walk up in the spot with me. That has to be one of my Spelman sisters."

"And why is that?"

"Because, that's how we roll."

I laugh out loud at Gia's gangstaness. "Okay. I will go with you, but I'm not staying out all night. I've got a morning class."

"Your bad! My first class isn't until eleven, so I can sleep in."

"Well, I'm taking a quick shower, and then I'll get dressed. What did you decide on?"

"This Tweety tee, black leggings, and heels. What do you think?"

I cock my head to one side and smile. "Fiyah!"

"Go shower! Quickly!"

And I do. Shower expeditiously that is. I'm actually getting in the mood to go out with my new friend. I sing in the shower, my new song, and think about Sam while getting fresh and clean.

When I emerge from the bathroom in my tiny robe,

smelling like Vanilla Coconut from Bath and Body Works, Piper and Meagan have joined the fray and are posted on Gia's bed between the mounds of clothing.

Piper is wearing skinny jeans, a glittery tank top, and heels with her hair pulled up in a side ponytail, looking retro den a mug. Meagan is much more sophisticated in her designer skirt, panty hose heels, and fitted button-down blouse. Her pin-straight, shoulder-length hair is pinned up on one side and the only makeup she has on is lip gloss.

"Don't just stand there gawking at us," Meagan says. "Get some clothes on, so we can go."

I haphazardly pick an outfit, a jean skirt and a dressy T-shirt. They can go on somewhere with those heels. Not me. I'm rocking some dressy flat sandals. They will be regretting those heels tonight when they're all blistered up, trying to look cute.

"So, I guess I'm driving, huh?" I ask the question with the obvious answer.

"Or we can take the party bus," Piper says.

"What is a party bus?" Meagan asks. "And why does it sound ghetto?"

Gia giggles. "That all depends on your definition of ghetto. It's a big fifty-five-passenger bus that picks us up for the party, in front of our dorms and it drops us off."

"You mean like a Greyhound bus?" Meagan has a distasteful look on her face, like she just smelled a whiff of day-old armpit funk.

Piper says, "It discourages drunk driving."

"Which I will not be doing because I don't drink," I reply. "I'm driving, so let's go!"

We prance out of me and Gia's room like we're ready to take on all of Atlanta. Like we're the flyest girls on campus.

As we cross the courtyard to the parking lot, I ask, "Whose party is this anyway? Are we invited?"

"Chi Kappa Psi," Meagan explains. "The Morehouse chapter. And yeah, everyone is invited."

Gia claps her hands with glee. "My first fraternity party! I am so stoked."

"I didn't want to go at first," Meagan says. Her high heels click on the pavement, punctuating her sentence. "But then again, this is Chi Kappa! I'm destined to be with a Chi Kappa."

"Why is that?" I ask as we pile into my car. This time Gia scores the coveted shotgun position.

"Chi Kappa are the brothers of Gamma Phi Gamma," Piper explains. "My foster dad is a Chi Kappa."

"My *real* dad is a Chi Kappa Psi man," Meagan boasts. "They always have the first party of the year."

"Where is the party?" I ask once I realize that I'm driving with absolutely no idea where I'm going.

Gia reads the flyer. "It says, The Mansion. Is that a club?"

"No," I reply. "It's a real mansion that gets rented out for parties. It's close by. I've been to a Mansion party or two and normally there's lots of alcohol and nobody checking ID."

"That's what's up," Piper says.

When all she hears is crickets, Piper says, "What? Why y'all looking at me like I'm a Lifetime movie waiting to happen?"

"Listen here, Piper," I say. "Everywhere I go, someone is snapping pictures to go on Mediatakeout.com. So if you're trying to get slizzard, you need to do that with a different crew."

Gia chimes in. "My mama would come all the way to Atlanta and kick my butt if she saw me on the Internet even looking like I'm thinking about getting drunk. Gwen does not roll like that."

"You call your mother Gwen?" Piper asks.

"Only behind her back," Gia replies. "She brings the ruckus."

Meagan says, "If you plan on pledging Gamma Phi Gamma, I suggest you carry yourself like a lady at all times."

Piper slumps back in her seat as if we've taken all the wind from her sails. I don't know about Meagan and Gia, but I will cut this chick loose with the quickness. We ain't Spelman sisters yet.

I've already got enough drama.

Gia says, "That doesn't mean we can't have fun though!"

I glance at Piper through the rearview mirror and she's gazing out the window with a sad expression on her face. I hope we didn't come down too hard on her. I'm just so over ridiculousness.

Gia and Meagan must feel the same way because we're all sitting here in silence, but I know the perfect thing to break up the monotony.

"Y'all want to hear my new single?" I ask.

Piper replies, "I have your entire album, Sunday. Which song is it?"

"I have it too," Gia says. "Tell me it's one of the slow cuts. Those are my favorites."

"It's 'The Highlight.' My favorite track on the whole record."

"That's my favorite too," Gia says. "It kinda became me and my boyfriend's song over the summer."

Meagan says, "Sounds like I need to purchase your CD."

I press the button on the CD player. "Yeah, you need to cop this. Fo sho."

It's funny, I think we all use an extra amount of slang when we talk to Meagan because she insists on being prep-school proper.

The music fills the car with Gia and Piper singing along. They both have cringe-worthy voices, but it makes me feel incredibly proud that they memorized my song.

"So what did you think?" I ask Meagan when the song is over.

"Well, it's not really my kind of music. I prefer Esperanza Spalding or classical. That said, it does have a beautiful melody."

Piper says, "Really? Girl, bye! Just say you like it."

This definitely breaks up the bad feelings in the car, because now we're all laughing.

"I'm doing a video shoot for the song on Saturday. Do y'all want to come with me? It's at Zillionaire's house."

"Zillionaire?" Gia asks.

"The rapper?" Piper finishes the question.

"Yes. Friday I learn the choreography, and Saturday we shoot."

"That's what's up," Piper says. "I am so there."

"Count me in too," Gia says.

When Meagan says nothing, both Gia and Piper glare at her.

She says, "What? I'm going shopping on Saturday with some upperclass ladies from Gamma Phi Gamma."

"Wow! And you didn't ask me to roll? You know I want to pledge," Piper says.

Meagan throws up a dismissive hand wave to Piper. "We can't even pledge our freshman year. Plus, I'm legacy, so I don't have to pledge. They're like my big sisters already."

"What does legacy mean?" Gia asks.

"It means that since my mother was a Gamma that I'm automatically in."

I roll my eyes at this incessant chatter about Gamma Phi Gamma. I have never been so glad to reach my destination. Meagan is cool, but she gets on my nerves with all that pampered-princess crap.

"*This* is the Mansion?" Gia asks. "Oh my gravy! It's incred! Me likee!"

I laugh out loud at Gia! Her slanguage is a little bit geek, a little bit hood, and a little bit country. Who says "oh my gravy"?

The Mansion is pretty impressive though. It's a huge round building constructed with concrete and glass. The glass is tinted for privacy, but it still gives the house a glam effect.

I feel like I'm underdressed! Maybe I should've asked where the party would be before I picked out my outfit. They even have valet parking!

After I hand over my keys, we strut to the front door,

probably looking like the crew of innocent, naive freshmen that we are. And check it out, there are two bouncers at the door, just like we're at the club.

"ID?" one of them asks.

We all pull out driver's licenses and promptly get the arm band that says *Toddler*. This is funny to me. Why we gotta be toddlers? Why can't we just be the fly underage girls?

"I thought you said they wouldn't be checking ID," Piper says.

I shrug. "I guess I was wrong."

Actually, I've only ever been to industry parties here. With those parties, it's anything goes. I guess they don't play that with college frat parties.

"There's my boyfriend!" Gia squeals as she dashes away from us. So much for Spelman sisterhood! She's dropped me in thirty seconds flat and left me with the Gamma groupies.

I would've dipped too, though, if my very hot boyfriend was at this party. Because there are a bunch of video vixen types who don't seem to have enough clothing on.

I watch as Gia gives her man a hug. He looks so happy to see her, even though I'm sure it hasn't been long since they hung out.

It makes me miss Sam terribly.

"Who is the hottie with Gia's boyfriend?" Piper asks.

Meagan says, "Maybe that's her Morehouse bestie. Let's go get introduced."

Could these two be anymore thirsty? I guess maybe I'd be joining in with the thirstiness if I didn't have a boyfriend.

Gia holds out her hand to us as we approach.

"These are my new friends that I was telling you about," Gia gushes. Must she be so excited about *everything?*

"O-M-G!" Kevin says. "You didn't say you were friends with Sunday Tolliver! Hi! I'm Kevin!"

On closer inspection, Gia's other friend Kevin is good looking, but he's definitely not a hottie in my book. Well, not in the traditional sense of hotties. He's lacking a great deal in the swag department. I would never kick it with a guy who spells out O-M-G, but that's just me.

I extend a hand to shake his. "Nice meeting you, Kevin. This is Piper and Meagan; they go to Spelman with us too."

I thought I'd go ahead and handle the introductions because Gia and her boyfriend are whispering and giggling about something they don't share. Yeah. They're disgusting.

"Oh right," Gia says, finally rejoining the conversation. "What she said. My cousin Hope was coming, but she changed her mind. Y'all will have to meet her later. And this is my boyfriend, Ricky. Ricky meet Sunday, Piper, and Meagan."

Ricky gives us a huge smile. Whoa. He is incredibly fine! Gia better hold on tight, because I can see the vultures already circling.

"Nice meeting y'all," Ricky says. "Come on, Gi-Gi. Let's go dance."

"That's what I'm talking about!" Gia says as she follows Ricky out to the area in the middle of the living room where everyone is dancing.

Kevin sighs. "They always abandon me for the dance floor. It's been like this since the ninth grade!"

"Don't worry," Meagan says. "We'll keep you company, right, Piper?"

Piper grins. "Sure. You're a cutie!"

Kevin's eyes widen. "You Spelman ladies are . . . aggressive."

"No, sweetie. *She's* aggressive," Meagan says while pointing at Piper. "I'm assertive. Did you happen to see where they're serving beverages?"

Kevin points across the room. "The non-alcoholic beverages are over there." He holds both of his arms out for Piper and Meagan to grab. "Shall we?" he says.

"We'll be back, Sunday. You want something?" Piper asks.

I shake my head. "Nah. I'm straight."

I spy out a chill place to sit near the back of the room. It's hard to explain, but although I like being on stage when I sing, I'm really a background chick in real life.

I get comfortable at my post and watch Gia and Ricky dance. They are really good. Her moves are sort of a mixture of old-school Aaliyah with Ciara thrown in. And Ricky reminds me of Columbus Short in *Stomp the Yard*. He dances hard and smooth at the same time.

"Lookie here! Goody Good decided to come out of her dorm!"

I look up at my cousin Dreya and release a sigh. Why is she at a frat party? She's not in college, so how would she even know about it? Plus, doesn't she have an album to record, or a small animal to terrorize?

"Dreya."

"Well, dang, cuzzo! You don't look happy to see me. I'm hurt."

I roll my eyes and check out Dreya's crew. One of the girls is a serious tomboy. She's got her hair pulled back in a low ponytail and she's wearing a tank top and some boyfriend jeans. The only thing that saves her from looking severely thugged out is that she has a fly designer bag and some fierce heels. The other girl with Dreya has interesting. . . . no . . . *impossible* body proportions. Her boobs are like three times the size of mine and I've got more than a handful. Her waist is unnaturally tiny like a Bratz doll, and her behind is gargantuan. I almost want to poke it to see if it's real.

"Drama, introduce us to your cousin," the tomboy says.

"Okay, dang! Y'all don't have to be so amped to meet her. She's just Sunday."

"She's an artist with a gold debut record," tomboy says. "I don't know what you smoking, Drama!"

"Okay," bootylicious says. "I might could be in her next video."

Dreya shakes her head with irritation. "You so stupid! Why would she have you in her video? She needs hot boys—not hot girls."

"It could happen! Sunday, I'm Tasia."

Tomboy sits down next to me. "And I'm Kiki. Rapper slash producer slash choreographer. Get at me. Follow me on Twitter."

"Um . . . okay," I say. "Nice to meet y'all."

"I wonder what Auntie Shawn would say about you kicking it at the same parties as me," Dreya says.

I laugh out loud. "Nothing, 'cause I'm grown."

Kiki high-fives me. "I know that's right."

Dreya moves Kiki out of the way and plops down next to me, crowding my space. This party just went from classy to ghetto in five minutes. Who let Dreya in? I thought they had bouncers at the door.

"So, I need you to write me another song," Dreya says. "That other stuff you gave me is too vanilla. And I want to rap."

"You want to rap?" I ask this incredulously even as I let myself entertain the idea of Dreya rapping. She might just be a good fit for that. I can see her spitting on a microphone. She's definitely got the attitude to pull it off, and she's got the vocals to sing her own hooks.

"What does Epsilon Records think about you rapping? That's a big change for you."

"I think they'll like it if it's hot. And then . . . well we won't be competing with one another all the time. This could be my thing."

The only thing that concerns me is that rappers, emcees, etc., have like this code and it ain't cool if you don't write your own lyrics. That could be the kiss of death to a rap career.

"Do you want to take a stab at composing your own lyrics? That might be best."

Dreya laughs out loud. "Girl, please. I'm not trying to sound all Dr. Seuss up in this piece. I want the fiyah."

I consider this again. Dilly and I could probably come up with some hotness for the mess that is Drama. Dilly is an up-and-coming rapper with Epsilon Records and he's got mad skills.

"Well, I've got a video shoot on Saturday."

"Where they shooting your video?"

"At Zac's mansion."

Dreya makes eye contact with Tasia and Kiki.

"See what I mean, y'all?" she says. "They show her mad love. It's like I'm a stepchild."

"Don't worry, ma," Kiki says. "Your time is coming."

I shake my head, because I know there's no convincing Dreya otherwise. She believes what she believes about how Epsilon Records treats us. Dreya doesn't realize that drama gets old sometimes, and it doesn't always sell records.

"Let's hook up on Sunday," I say, "Oh wait. Dang, I've got a recording session with Bethany."

"All day?" Dreya asks.

"No, but I have to write a paper this weekend. Sunday evening will be my only chance."

Dreya sucks her teeth and rolls her eyes. "Well, dang, cuzzo. Just when can I get on your calendar?"

"Monday evening."

"All right then, princess!" Dreya says as she stands.

"What do you mean?" Her words didn't sound like a compliment. It sounded like a diss.

"It means that if you don't get out from under Mystique's shadow, you always gonna be her successor, and she ain't giving up that queen throne. Come on, y'all, let's be out. I got what I came for."

I guess Dreya forgot who I am or what I came to do. I'm not in the music industry for anyone's queendom. I'm in this game to pay for my college and help turn my mother's trife life to lavish.

I scan the crowd to see what's up with my friends. Piper has abandoned Kevin and Meagan and is on the dance floor, getting it poppin' all by herself. I guess she got tired of waiting for someone to ask her to dance.

Meagan and Kevin look like they're having a serious conversation. Way too serious for this party. They look like they're having some type of world summit for young black leaders.

And Gia and Ricky have a little audience now. Some of the Gamma Phi Gamma girls are whistling and the Chi Kappa Psi brothers are yelling, "Go 'head!"

Gia's Tweety shirt is stuck to her body and her face is glistening with sweat. Ricky looks overheated too. I know where to find some backup dancers in a pinch, because they are crowd pleasers.

A satisfied grin appears on my face as my song "Can U See Me" blasts from the speakers. This is exactly what I thought college would be like. New friends, hot parties, and my music.

Piper runs over to me and grabs my hand. "I know you're enjoying holding up the wall, but you've got to dance on this!"

I allow Piper to pull me to the dance floor. This is truly what's up! If I was writing my own dream, I couldn't make it better than this!

4

My least favorite task to complete as a pop star is shooting videos. It is so much work and not even the least bit fun. First, I have to learn choreography. I'm an okay dancer, but nothing like Mystique and she always has complex moves. At least "The Highlight" is a slow song, so I don't have to pop, lock, and drop it.

"This is what a plié looks like, Sunday."

I watch the dance instructor, Tina, do a graceful knee bend and come back to a standing position.

I don't know if I can accomplish that. Especially in front of everyone in Zac's dance studio. The mirrors on the walls are supposed to be good for dancers, but to me they are just intimidating.

"Come on, Sunday," Mystique says. "You have to at least try."

I glance over at the guy who is supposed to be my leading man in this video. His name is DeShawn, and he is ridiculously cute. He's dark brown with a low cut fade, full lips, and big expressive eyes. He's also ripped with muscles, probably because he's on the football team at Georgia State.

DeShawn's eyes sparkle as he grins at me. "Come on, Ms. Tolliver. We don't have all day," he teases.

"Oh shut up!" I reply with a chuckle. "You come over here and try it if it's so easy."

DeShawn swaggers to the center of the room, clears his throat, and shocks everyone, especially me, with the perfect plié.

"Now what?" he asks as I stand there with my mouth hanging open.

Mystique bursts into laughter. "Um, DeShawn here is messing with you. He is a classically trained dancer! He's probably been doing pliés since he was little."

"Both of my parents are dancers," he explains. "They met in the Alvin Ailey Dance Company."

"Okay, so? I can't dance," I say.

"Yes, you can!" Mystique says.

Gia and Piper chant from their post on the wall. "Yes, you can. Yes, you can. Yes, you can."

"Okay, dag!" I say as I try to get my mind right.

It's just one move. One little knee bend. I can do this without looking awkward, right?

I take a deep breath, and try to accomplish the move. It looks okay to me in the mirror, but I don't know if I did it right.

"Almost," the choreographer says. "I need your back a little straighter."

I let out a loud and frustrated sigh, and everyone in the room bursts into laughter.

"Try it again, Sunday," DeShawn says. "You want me to do it with you? Let me help."

DeShawn takes my arms and places them in the air, and then puts his hand in the small of my back. I ignore the tingle that goes through me, because I have a boyfriend, and no other boy (no matter how fine he might be) should make me feel tingly.

"Now go," DeShawn says. "My hand will help keep your back straight."

This time when I do the plié, Tina and Mystique clap! DeShawn takes a bow and a smile bursts onto my face.

"That was a perfect plié," Tina says. "I'd think you'd taken ballet your entire life."

"Finally!" I say. "Can we take a break now? I need some water!"

Tina looks at Mystique and Mystique nods. "Okay, take five," Tina says.

I rush over to the refreshment table, but instead of water I choose a bottle of apple juice. Gia, Piper, and De-Shawn all join me although I'm ashamed to look at De-Shawn right now with that plié debacle still looming over my head.

"I don't know if you had anything to do with the se-lection," DeShawn says to me as he pops open a can of Sprite, "but good looking out! I'm paying my way through school with modeling gigs, so this could really open up some doors for me."

"I didn't have anything to do with it, but I hope it's a

come-up for you. You're pretty talented." And fine. But I do not say this out loud, because I have a boyfriend.

"You're on the football team with my boyfriend, Ricky," Gia says. "Do you know him?"

DeShawn nods. "Yes, he's the freshman that everyone is ranting and raving about. The first-string quarterback is pretty nervous, because he had a rough season last year, and is already struggling a little bit."

"Well, Ricky would never come in trying to take somebody's spot. He would wait for his own time to shine."

"That's good to know," DeShawn says. "But that won't stop coach from making the move if need be. Trust, if Gray fumbles that ball one more time on a game-changing play, your boyfriend will see some action."

Gia has a contemplative look on her face. I like how she has her boyfriend's back at all times. She's not even fazed at DeShawn's good looks. She's holding a conversation with him like he's some regular dude. I could learn a thing or two from her, I think, about being a good girlfriend.

But then again, her man isn't across the country, on a college campus full of beautiful girls, and kicking it with Zac the Zillionaire. It's hard for me to imagine Sam not doing a double take when a cutie with a booty walks past him.

Why couldn't he have stayed here and continued working for Big D?

When Zac made Sam the offer to work at Epsilon Record's main office in New York, as an in-house producer/songwriter, it took me some time to get used to the idea that he wouldn't be here. To be honest, I still don't know if I'm used to it.

But, the opportunity was one that he couldn't pass up. He deserves to blow up just like anybody else. As a matter of fact, Dreya, her bootleg ex-boyfriend, Truth, and I wouldn't even have record deals if it wasn't for Sam's talent.

"So, are you seeing anyone?" DeShawn asks as if he's reading my thoughts about my long-distance love. "I remember seeing something on Sandra Rose, about you dating this rapper?"

I roll my eyes. "I never dated Truth. That was my cousin."

"So you're single?"

"No, I'm not. I do have a boyfriend. He goes to school in New York."

"So, out of sight, out of mind?" DeShawn asks. He punctuates his question by biting his bottom lip. Dude's mack game is on point, that's for sure.

I give him a little smile. "Sorry. My boo is always on my mind."

Gia and Piper say, "Awwwww . . ." in unison.

"That's too bad. Let me know if you need an escort anywhere. I'd love to have you on my arm."

"Why? Will it help your modeling career?" I ask. Once I say the question, I wish I could take it back. DeShawn looks offended.

"It probably would, but that's not why I said it. I think you're fly, Sunday. Can't fault a brotha for trying."

Mystique calls from the dance floor. "Come on, y'all.

Let's nail this so we don't have to be here until two o'clock in the morning."

DeShawn and I hustle back to the dance floor, but my mind isn't totally on learning dance moves. I'm thinking about DeShawn's offer to escort me somewhere. Is there something wrong with me that I'm actually giving a second thought to his offer? I shake my head and concentrate on the choreography, because even though DeShawn is a straight hottie, I know I'd be ready to spazz all the way out if Sam was even thinking of giving another girl some play.

At the end of the song, DeShawn has to step in and hug me from behind. Feeling his arms around me is a distraction, just like the butterflies in my stomach.

I let out a big sigh as the song ends. This long-distance teenage love affair is going to be a lot harder than I thought.

5

It's late Saturday night and we finally finished up my video shoot. I'm tired like a big dawg, but still hungry, so Gia, Piper, Meagan, and I decide to make a stop at Waffle House before heading back to our dorm.

"I'm glad I decided to come to your video shoot," Meagan says. "It was so less ghetto than I thought it would be."

Gia bursts into laughter and spits water across the table. "Why did you think it would be ghetto?"

"Why did she admit that she thought it would be ghetto?" I ask. "Meagan, you are a trip!"

Meagan laughs too, as she takes a sip of her hot tea. Only Meagan would come into Waffle House late on a Saturday night and order hot tea.

"I thought it would be ghetto because of those reality shows, Sunday. You know that was a hot ghetto mess if there ever was one."

I nod in agreement. I think about the first reality show that I filmed with Truth, Dreya, Bethany, and Dilly. There was drama on top of drama happening on a daily basis. Luckily, I wasn't in the center of it all. It helped me with Epsilon Records that I came across as the "positive" one. I even got my own reality show special that they finished filming on my first day of college.

"The first one was pretty wretched," I say, "but the one we just filmed with my video shoot for 'Can U See Me' is pretty good. There's only a tiny, tiny bit of drama, but it's really quite watchable."

Piper smiles at me and shakes her head. "Don't you just sound like a BET commercial."

"Whatever, loser!" I tear the bottom of the wrapper off my straw and blow so that the paper flies in Piper's direction.

"Was any of the stuff about you and that rapper guy true?" Gia asks. "He doesn't seem like your type at all. All of those tattoos and those dingy tanks."

"Um, no. Let me repeat that! Hecks to tha no! Truth was my cousin's boyfriend, and he's an abusive little punk."

Gia, Piper, and Meagan all wince at the word "abusive." I guess none of us like the idea of getting hurt by a boyfriend. For the life of me, I can't figure out why Dreya won't leave him alone. Even after she got jumped by a bunch of girls, supposedly at Truth's request, she still deals with him. One of the bloggers took pictures of them hugged up in Club Pyramids—the last club in Atlanta anyone will ever find me.

"So that guy in your video is totally hot. Is he single?" Meagan asks. "Does he go to Morehouse?"

"He goes to Georgia State," Gia replies. "He plays ball with Ricky."

Meagan scrunches up her nose. "Never mind then. My guy has got to come from Morehouse."

"Don't you think that's a silly rule?" Piper asks. "Like what makes the guys at Morehouse any better than the guys at Georgia State? A hottie is a hottie as far as I'm concerned."

Meagan rolls her eyes. "Seriously? There is a huge difference. Morehouse is an elite private university. They don't just accept everyone. You have to be a game changer to get in. Plus my mother went to Spelman and my dad went to Morehouse. Enough said. This is my destiny."

All three of us give her blank stares.

"Oh good grief!" Meagan says. "Why don't you all give *her* the blank stare for drooling over every black boy that she sees? You're one of those white chicks that only dates black guys aren't you, Piper? You might as well be a Kardashian."

Ouch! That stung me and it wasn't even meant for me. I don't even get that vibe from Piper anyway, so Meagan is way out of line with her accusation.

Piper says, "That's not me, Meagan. I like hot boys in every shade. I don't discriminate."

"I'll believe that when I see you drooling over a white boy," Meagan says.

Gia frowns at Meagan. It looks like somebody's

mama's frown. "Why does it even matter? There are more than enough boys to go around."

Meagan shrugs. "Whatever. I have my opinion, you have yours. Let's agree to disagree."

Several members of Gamma Phi Gamma walk up to our table, wearing their signature color, turquoise. Meagan sits up straight and beams a smile in their direction, but they're focusing on Gia.

"Hello, ladies!" the shorter of the two girls says. "I'm Peony, and this is Sharday."

I know a peony is a flower, but this girl has a ridiculously long weave on her head and the first thought that pops into my mind is *pony* as in horsey hair, instead of Peony. Plus her big wide-set eyes kind of remind you of staring a horse in the face.

Sharday is the prettier of the girls. She's a dark ebony beauty with a wild afro held off her face by a headband. She doesn't need any makeup, but she's wearing just a touch of lip gloss.

"We saw you at the Chi Kappa Psi party," Sharday says to Gia. "You are a really good dancer. Do you know how to step as well?"

"I do. I used to be the captain of the Hi-Steppers squad in my high school."

Peony's smile stretches across her face to reveal very long white teeth. "We'll just have to remember that when it's time for new member intake. We could always use a talented stepper for the big step show in the spring."

"Well, girls, enjoy your waffles," Sharday says. "We've got to get back to our boyfriends. We just wanted to say hello."

"Hello, Big Sister Sharday and Big Sister Peony!" Meagan says like a soldier.

Both Sharday and Peony give Meagan tight smiles and sashay back over to their table, where they've got two very cute guys, obviously from Morehouse because they're wearing their shirts and ties like they just came from church.

Piper covers her mouth with her hand to contain her giggles. "They just dissed you, Meagan! Are your big sisters not really feeling you?"

"Whatever!" Meagan replies. "They did not diss me! They spoke to all of us."

"But obviously they came over here to get at Gia," Piper says. "Sounded like recruitment to me, although we can't even pledge until next year."

"It doesn't make me any difference one way or the other," Gia says. "My cousin Hope is like my sister anyway. I don't need a sorority."

I listen to Gia and I'm glad that she's my friend. I hope that we get to feel like sisters too.

"No matter what, I will be a Gamma Phi Gamma. Even if Big Sister Sharday and Big Sister Peony aren't feeling me," Meagan says. "It's called legacy, girls."

Gia, Piper, and I reply in unison. "We know!"

6

"*You stressed/steady tryin' to rumble wit da best/Sweetie, I'm blessed, passed every test/I like you less and less 'cause every time I see/you be talkin' mess, talkin' like people wanna be you/You? Who? A second-rate emcee?/You get less props from me than I give to my enemies.*"

Something isn't right about how Dreya is delivering these lyrics. There's something too *girly* about it. Not that a rapper can't be feminine, but she's too feminine.

"Dreya, I want you to really think about what you're saying," I say. "These lines are disses, and you're saying it like it's a nursery rhyme."

"I'm trying to remember the words."

"Look at the paper. You can worry about remembering them later. I need to hear some attitude in your delivery."

Big D sits in the corner of the lab, his room in the studio where Sam and I usually create. Dilly is here too, and he's sporting a new look. A curly Mohawk that really flatters his face. I think it's because his hair, eyebrows, and eyelashes are so dark, but it's really working for him.

"Pretend that you're spitting the lyrics at Truth," Dilly says. "That should help you find some attitude."

I roll my eyes, but keep my peace on the subject of Truth. She *can't* say it like she's saying it to Truth, because she's still messing with that dude.

"Truth is still her boyfriend," I say, wondering if everyone can hear the irritation in my voice. "So try someone else, like an enemy. Maybe Bethany."

Big D stands from his chair looking like a big ol' brown Incredible Hulk. "You're back with him, Drama? What are you thinking?"

"I am not back with him," Dreya replies. "So y'all can stop tripping."

"Really? Then why are y'all on Twitter sending each other pictures and stuff?" I ask. "Cut the games, Dreya. Y'all are back together."

Big D says, "You want to be real careful with that, baby girl. Zac and Mystique aren't feeling him, and his time is up at Epsilon Records."

"So what? Epsilon Records is not the only company out here signing record deals. Truth just got signed to Big Cash Gents Records, so he's gonna be a'ight."

My eyes widen at the mention of Big Cash Gents Records. They are known for gangsta activity. The rumor in the industry is that they got started with money from drug deals. Getting let go from Epsilon was not a good look, but signing up with Big Cash Gents is an even worse look.

"Let's get back to this record," Dreya fusses. "I'm trying to figure out my career right now anyway. I need to make sure I've got something popping off at the end of the day."

"Okay, try the phrase again," I say. "Bring the attitude."

This time Dreya gets in a zone or something, because she brings the fiyah! She spits every line like she means it. Like she's really got a vendetta with someone. She totally makes me believe it. Big D and Dilly like it too, because they both give her a round of applause when she's done.

Dreya takes a little bow and smiles. "Who said I can't be a female emcee?"

"It wasn't me!" Dilly says, as he gives Dreya a fist pound. "You did that, girl. I felt that!"

"So now the only ones left to convince are the executives at Epsilon Records," Big D says. "But I think if you go hard for your whole record like you did right there, you won't have a problem convincing them."

Dreya smiles hard, and I can't help but share her joy. It's not often that I get to see Dreya totally happy. We grew up like sisters, most of the time in the same house, and it seems like we were always competing. This is something that she gets to have all to herself. She never has to worry about me rapping. Even though I'm nice on the mic, I enjoy singing so much more.

"Do you think Epsilon Records would let me do a duet with Dilly?" Dreya asks.

"You want me to do a duet with you? That's what's up!"

Big D says, "I'm sure they would. They're still trying to figure out how to put Dilly on the map."

My phone rings, and I'm sure my face lights up when I see the caller ID. It's Sam! With the video shoot, I haven't talked to him all weekend.

"Hey, Sam," I say in a voice that is just a little bit too bubbly.

"Hey, Sunday. Are you alone right now?"

Okay, he sounds weird. "No. I'm in the lab with Big D, Dilly, and Dreya." I hold the phone up in the air. "Say hey to Sam, y'all."

Big D says, "You need to get back to the A. We've got work to do, son."

I place the phone back on my face. "What's up?"

"Do me a favor and go upstairs for a second, so I can talk to you in private."

Now, he's scaring me. "Is everything okay?"

"Yes, it's okay, but I just want to tell you this without everyone seeing your face."

"Okay. I'll be back, y'all."

I take the steps two at a time, because Sam's tone sounds anxious, and he's such a cool dude. He hardly ever gets wound up.

Huffing and puffing at that little bit of physical exertion, I ask, "Okay, what's going on?"

"I don't know how to say this, so I'm just gonna say it. I went to a party with Zac over the weekend, and some things popped off that I wish never did."

"What *kind* of things?"

I hear Sam sigh over the phone. Not a good sign.

"Well, I wasn't drinking. At all. I was sipping on a Coke. But someone slipped something in my soda when I set it down."

"What? That's crazy! Are you okay?"

"Yes, I'm fine. But after the party, Zac told me it was ground-up ecstasy."

Ecstasy? Oh my goodness! My mother always told me to always buy my own drink and never set it down. Number-one rule of going to parties with strangers. Number two, leave with who I came there with. Sam needs to go to the Shawn Tolliver school of kicking it.

"You should be glad you didn't get hurt. I'm glad nothing happened to you," I say. "Next time, you should be more careful with your drink!"

"Well . . . I wouldn't say that nothing happened."

"What do you mean?"

Sam clears his throat. A stall tactic.

"What do you mean, Sam?" I ask again, this time my tone of voice a little louder and harsher.

"Zac told me that I made out with a girl on the dance floor."

I drop the phone. Hear the screen on my Android shatter, but I don't care.

After I take a deep breath and blow it out, I pick up the wounded phone. "Come again?"

"Don't make me say it again, Sunday. It was hard enough to say it the first time."

"Come *again*?"

"I kissed a girl. Don't know who she was or her name. Zac said I should tell you, because there was someone there taking pictures and it'll probably be on the Internet."

"Zac told you to tell me? You didn't think that was information I'd like to know? You're all the way in New York City, playing tonsil Twister with some skank, and *Zac* had to tell you to man up and let me know?"

"Sunday. You are overreacting. I can't even tell you what the chick looks like."

"But everyone on Mediatakeout.com will know tomorrow. You know they get like a million hits a day?"

I press end on my shattered screen. I can't listen to his voice another minute. How can he say that I'm overreacting? He would sooo not be saying that if the shoe was on the other foot. I know, because we've already been down this path when Truth was trying to push up on me. I wasn't giving Truth any play, but Sam still went into trip-out mode.

Sam calls right back. I don't answer. I click decline and send that joint to voice mail. Do not want to continue this conversation.

Two seconds later he calls again. I do the same thing.

On the third time, I pick up.

"Sam, do not keep calling me."

"I'm gonna keep calling until you talk to me."

"Then I'ma have to block your number."

"Don't block my number."

"Then don't keep calling me."

I hear Sam sigh. He doesn't have the right to sigh. After a few moments of silence and breathing, I disconnect the call again.

I'm beyond angry. Trying to feel this with an emotion

other than rage and I'm coming up short. Even though I know he didn't do it on purpose. Even though the girl is some faceless, nameless groupie. Well, she's faceless and nameless now. She won't be tomorrow or the next day when someone decides to put Sam on blast to the Internet community.

Somebody right now is probably saying, "Tweet that" on a picture of Sam lip-locked on the dance floor. It makes me sick to my stomach. I swear, technology is a blessing and a curse.

I try to compose myself before going back downstairs, but I'm sure Dreya and Big D are going to know something is up immediately. Why didn't Sam wait to tell me this when I got back to the privacy of my dorm? He wanted to clear his conscience, I suppose, but now he's gonna have me answering questions that I don't want to answer.

"What's wrong with you?" Dreya asks as I reenter the basement studio area.

"Nothing. I'm straight."

Big D says, "You are definitely not straight, but I know better than to press you when you're not trying to talk about something."

"Ooh, what did Sam do?" Dreya asks, ignoring Big D's declaration. "Did he break up with you for some New York video vixen? Do we need to go to NYC and regulate? He's got some nerve with his ugly self! How he gonna play you and he ain't even cute?"

I shake my head and frown. "Sam did not play me! Not really. Someone slipped him a drug at the club, and he kissed some girl."

"And he told you?" Dilly asks. "Did he think you'd be okay with that?"

"Do you believe him?" Big D asks.

"Yeah, I do, but I'm still heated."

"And you should be, because he's probably lying," Dreya says. "Ain't nobody slip him nothing. He was doing the slipping. Slipping his tongue in another girl's mouth, and now he's just trying to cover his tracks."

Big D frowns at Dreya and says, "Sam isn't like that. If he wanted to break up with you he'd do it. He's not that guy, Sunday."

"Every guy is *that* guy if they have the opportunity."

I feel angry with myself for letting the tears fall. Especially in front of Dreya, who seems to gain strength off my unhappiness like some kind of super villain who thrives on negativity.

"I don't know if you care what I think," Dilly says, "but I don't believe Sam would cheat on you. First of all, you're hot. Second of all, you're Sunday Tolliver! That's like the ultimate come-up for him."

"For every fly chick in the world, there's a dude that's tired of her and on to the next one."

Dreya reminds me of that little grey stuffed animal on *Winnie the Pooh*. Was he a donkey? The one who was always saying, "Oh bother" and raining on everyone's parade.

"That's enough, Drama," Big D says. "You sound a whole lot like misery loving company right now."

Dreya snatches her purse and puts on her sunglasses (even though it's dark outside) and starts walking toward the steps.

"I'm out of here. If you want to be in denial, Sunday, that's on you. I hope it all works out for you."

I scowl and plop down on Big D's comfortable leather sectional as Dreya sashays out of the basement. Just like I said . . . she loves to rain on everybody's parade.

Big D opens his mouth to speak and I hold up my hand. "No, please don't say anything else about this. I have to deal with this in my way. No matter what, Sam is supposed to be my boyfriend. He knows that I'm in the public eye and that he can't do stuff to embarrass me. Whether I forgive him or not for being stupid has nothing to do with the fact that I will have to deal with the questions."

"Yeah, you're right, baby girl. I can't argue with you or defend Sam on that one."

Dilly says, "It's gonna be straight, Sunday."

"I need to get out of here. I've got a study session with my roommate. We've got a paper to write in our composition class for Thursday."

"Dang, Sunday," Dilly says. "You are going to wear yourself out."

"Nope. Not gonna. I'm getting a Frappuccino on the way back to the dorm."

"When are you inviting me to the campus to meet all of your hot friends?" Dilly asks.

"Ha! When you grow up! And stop acting like you don't have a girlfriend. Bethany would flip out if she heard you say that."

"Bethany and I are on a break. She's too much for me."

My eyes widen, and for a second I forget all about my drama. "What do you mean? What's up with y'all?"

"She's talking crazy! She told me she loves me and she wants me to move in with her. I'm like whoa! Hold up! I ain't even out of high school yet. I don't want to wife anyone."

"Yeah, that's tripped out. You want me to talk to her?" I ask. I'm not sure what I would say, but clearly she needs a reality check.

"Naw, I handled it," Dilly says. "I told her I wasn't ready for all that. I still have to go to prom! Plus, my sister would freak out if I tried to move in with Bethany."

"All right then." I jump up from the couch. "I'll holla at y'all later. Big D, do you need me in the studio to help record Bethany's album?"

He shakes his head. "No, ma. Focus on your studies. Mystique and I can handle the recording. You've done the hard part by writing the songs. Plus, you'll have a few promo events the next couple of weekends. Your single starts on the radio on Wednesday, and the video will be released in two weeks."

"When do I get to see the final cut of it?"

"Probably next Friday. I'll call you."

I give Big D and Dilly our customary hugs. "Okay then, get at me!"

Dilly says, "I'm gonna walk you out."

As we go upstairs, Dilly seems extra serious about something. Maybe he's got something more to get off his chest about Bethany.

I use the keyless entry to unlock my door, but Dilly rushes to open it for me. He's got great manners. Someone raised him right. I hate to think that it was his ghetto sister, Keisha, but maybe she did do something right.

"What's up?" I ask as I step in the car.

He shrugs, as he leans on my open car door. "Nothing. It just feels so different without you and Sam at the studio every day. I think Big D feels like y'all leaving him behind or something. He's been in trip-out mode lately."

"For real?"

"Yeah, and he and Shelly been having problems too."

Shelly is Big D's ex-video-vixen girlfriend. Shelly's been holding it down for Big D for years. She cooks, cleans, and is always on his arm at events. Always. But Big D has chicks on the side. I always wondered if she knew about them and just looked the other way or if she didn't know.

"Big D needs to do right by Shelly! She's a real ride-or-die-type chick, and she's incredibly fly. I wish I had her body."

Dilly laughs out loud. "You *could* have her body. Some of it's store bought, I think!"

We crack up laughing on this one. Shelly will never admit it, but her badonkadonk does not look like it grew naturally. That teeny, tiny waist she has does not seem like it was designed to hold up all that booty.

"She wants Big D to marry her," Dilly says. "But he's not sure."

"He better do the right thing!"

"Well, I think I'm breaking up with Bethany. I didn't want to say it in front of D, because he is against it. He wants us to be a media sweetheart couple, but she's too psycho."

"What do you mean, psycho?"

Even though Bethany and I haven't been close lately, we were best friends from elementary all the way through our senior year of high school. We'd probably still be friends if she hadn't hooked up with my ex-boyfriend Romell. I wasn't even feeling him anymore, but it was the principle of the matter. Too many boys in the world to go after your best friend's ex! But through all that, she's never done anything that I could call psycho.

"Well, she saw me at the club with a bunch of kids from school, and she got all amped up because I hadn't invited her. So, she took a bunch of my clothes that I had left in her car, and poured bleach all over them."

"Okay, yeah. That's pretty psycho."

"That's not all. She wrote me a letter saying that she doesn't think she can live without me, and that she might hurt herself if I leave her."

"For real? Wow, that's tripped out. You want me to talk to her?"

"No. I think I can handle it."

"You make sure you let me know if you want me to talk to her."

"You have enough on your plate, Sunday. I was just venting for a second. You just make sure you clear your schedule when it's time for my prom, 'cause I want you to be my date."

I laugh out loud. "That's how you ask a girl out?"

"That's how I ask *you* out. You owe me."

I guess he's right. Dilly was the pinch-hitter prom date for me, when Sam decided to act a fool. I can definitely do him the same favor.

"You just let me know what color dress to wear."

"That money-green dress you rocked to your prom will do just fine."

"Uh, no. A pop star never wears the same dress twice."

Dilly gives me a fist bump. "That you are, Sunday. I'm just glad I knew you before your head blew up."

I smile at Dilly as I close my car door and pull out of Big D's driveway. I am a pop star, no matter how I slice it. And I've got all the pop-star craziness that comes along with it.

I try to put Sam and his stupidity out of my mind. Time to focus on my alter ego, Sunday Tolliver, freshman at Spelman. My college life, so far, is pretty drama free, so that's where I'm about to hang out for a while.

A pop star needs a break every now and then.

7

Gia is sitting on her bed with a major frown on her face. She just got off the phone with the financial aid office, and although I tried not to dip, I overheard her asking them when her student loan refund check would be in. I guess they didn't tell her what she needed to hear.

"Is everything okay?" I ask.

Gia smiles. "Yes, I'm cool. I've got a full scholarship, so as long as my classes, books, and room and board are paid for, I'm straight. I just have to keep getting good grades."

"But if you need anything, please let me know."

She shakes her head. "Nope. Not gonna do it. I've got a rich uncle back home. I will hit him up before I saddle you with my lack of finances."

"Don't sisters take care of each other?" I ask.

"Yes, and I promise I will let you know if I have an

emergency. As of right now, as long as they keep making ramen noodles and Kool-Aid, I'm straight."

"Okay. I may have a couple of gigs for you and Ricky, though. I have to do a few shows over the next couple of weekends to promote my single. Plus it's almost time for the American Music Award nominations, so I need to stay in the public eye."

"What kind of gig?"

"Backup dancing. Y'all made it hot at the Chi Kappa party."

Gia nods. "And this is a paying gig?"

"Yes, of course!"

"That's what's up! And, I love the AMAs. Are you performing on the show?"

I shrug. "Not sure yet. But if I do, do you want to be a dancer?"

Gia jumps up from her bed, crashes onto mine, and hugs me tightly. "Pinch me! I think I'm dreaming! That would be absolutely, ridiculously incredible."

"You are not dreaming! I need you, girl, because I can't dance."

"I can help you with that. My cousin Hope was totally hopeless until I helped her."

I crack up. "Hope was hopeless!"

"Yes, she was, and stop laughing, because she's on her way over here! I don't want you to burst into laughter when you meet her!"

"Okay, I'll try to pull myself together."

Gia gives me a suspicious look. "You still look like you want to giggle. Think of something serious. What about

Meagan and Piper? Think about them. They are seriously getting on my nerves."

"They are? I haven't really talked to either of them in the last few days. Are they arguing or something?"

Gia shakes her head. "No, they are both trying to holler at my best friend Kevin."

"The one from Morehouse?"

"Yes. And he's not feeling either one of them. Kevin is not trying to have a girlfriend yet. Meagan scared him, and Piper is not really his type."

"Meagan scared him?" This is funny! Now I'm laughing again, and Gia was trying to make me stop.

"Yes, she was too aggressive. She started telling him how he needed to pledge Chi Kappa, and all about her plans to marry a Morehouse man."

"No, she didn't! That girl is a trip. Poor Kevin. But what's wrong with Piper? Why didn't he like her?"

"Well . . . Kevin is kind of old school, and she has too many tattoos. When he told me about her, all he said was, 'The blood of Jesus.'"

Now I'm howling with laughter. "Gia, you are making this worse! But at least I'm not laughing about your cousin anymore."

There's a knock on the door. That must be Hope.

"Pull yourself together!" Gia fusses.

Gia gets up to open the door, and her cousin Hope walks in. She and Gia look a lot alike. They have the same creamy tan skin, big eyes, and thick eyebrows. Hope is all about the pin-straight hair, though. She's Gia's hair opposite. And her clothing style is Juicy Couture from head to toe. I guess their faces are where the similarities end.

"Hopey Hope! What's good?" Gia asks as she hugs her cousin.

Hope shakes her head. "Gia, you are so not fixable!"

Gia grins at me. "She hates my nickname for her. It's too crunktastical for her."

Hope gives Gia a tight-lipped glare and shakes my hand. "Hi, Sunday. I'm Hope—not Hopey Hope—and I am a huge fan. It's such an honor to meet you."

"Same here! Gia can't stop talking about her favorite cousin."

This puts a huge smile on Hope's face. "That's sweet! She's lucky to have you as a roommate. My roommate is awful."

Hope sits down on Gia's beanbag chair. The chair that I hope to convince her to throw away at some point. It's lime green and actually pretty comfy, but it is not cute.

"What's wrong with her?" Gia asks.

"She is totally boy crazy. She's hooked up with three different guys already. I mean we haven't even been in school a month yet."

"Ewww!" Gia says. "She's probably a walking bacteria."

"I know, right! I saw a prescription on her bed for penicillin."

I bite my lip. "Well, she could've had any kind of infection. Could've been a tooth or something."

"True. I just hate having to hear her."

"Oh, now that's just nasty," I say. "That's pretty disgusting."

"Exactly. You should come over here when she starts tripping," Gia says.

"No can do. Freshmen have a one a.m. curfew until the second semester. So I just turn my iPod up!"

Gia turns her lips up into a "something in here stinks" pose. "Glad that ain't me."

"Right," I add. "I've got the perfect roomie!"

Gia hugs me again. "So do I."

Hope rolls her eyes. "I hate you both. But what is this I hear about Kevin getting major play?"

"Is that what he told you?" Gia asks. "He is funny. He's scared of both girls so I don't know what he's bragging about."

I'm enjoying this banter back and forth between Gia and Hope. They have the kind of relationship that I wish Dreya and I had. We could be like this. Laughing and sharing news. I bet Hope isn't gleeful when Gia has boyfriend issues.

"Can I ask y'all a question?" I ask.

"Yep," Gia says.

Hope says, "Sure."

"How do y'all get along so well? My cousin and I . . . well, we don't get along at all. I've always wanted us to be friends."

Hope and Gia break out into a flurry of giggles. And Hope finally answers, "We haven't always been friends. I couldn't stand Gia our freshman year of high school."

"She was mad that I was a better Hi-Stepper than she was."

Hope says, "She was mad that I had better hair." She punctuates this with a hair flip.

"I had not embraced my fro yet," Gia explains. "But now, I like mine better than yours."

"To each her own," Hope says.

Gia says, "At some point, you and Dreya will probably be really cool. Once she stops hating on your shine."

"You watched the reality show?" I ask.

Hope replies, "We watched every episode. She needs to get over herself."

This is true. Dreya does need to get over herself. I just hope her new rap career is what puts her on the map. I would hate to see her crash and burn doing this.

"She's going to put out a rap album," I say.

Gia frowns. "Not a fan of rap. At all."

"Me either," Hope says. "But I will listen to some of it."

My phone buzzes on the bed, and I pick it up. It's a text from Sam. **Miss u.** I frown and throw it down. Feeling real ambivalent toward him right now. Haven't talked to him since I was over Big D's.

I do not want to break up with him! Not at all. I really care about him, maybe I even love him. I'm not sure about that. But he keeps making me cry. I don't like crying at all. Aren't you supposed to smile uncontrollably when you're in love?

"Who is that?" Gia asks. "Because you've got a stanky look on your face all of a sudden."

"Nobody."

"Yikes. It must be Sam. You should forgive him, Sunday. What happened to him could've happened to any guy."

"Would you forgive Ricky if he did the same thing?"

Gia pauses for an extended moment. "I. Don't. Know."

"Exactly!"

"Clue me in," Hope says.

"My boyfriend, maybe soon-to-be-ex-boyfriend went to a club and he says someone slipped something in his drink."

"Oh my!" Hope says. "Did anything happen to him?"

"Yeah, another girl's tongue ended up down his throat."

"Ouchie! I don't know what I would do in that scenario either," Hope says. "I don't have a boyfriend right now, but still. I'd probably be really angry."

"I'm beyond angry. But he keeps apologizing."

Luckily the bloggers didn't get a hold of the picture. That would've made everything worse. But it's been a few days and the story hasn't surfaced yet. Maybe Zac threatened some people. He's good at that. His threats got Truth's record deal with Epsilon Records deep-sixed when Truth put his hands on Dreya. I thought it was kind of gangsta of Zac to do that, but if he did the same thing for Sam, then I actually appreciate it.

My phone buzzes again. I ignore it, because I know it's Sam.

Gia asks, "Are you going to check that?"

When I shake my head, she jumps up and snatches my phone off the bed before I can stop her.

"He says he's downstairs," she says after reading my text.

"What?"

I grab the phone so I can see for myself. When I see that Gia wasn't playing, I text him back. **Why and how are u here?**

I tap my foot on the floor as I wait for his reply. I don't even know if I want to see him right now. I want to hug him, but I want to kick him at the same time. See, I said I was ambivalent!

He texts back. **Zac bought me a ticket. I fly back on Friday. Will only miss one class.**

I text: **Oh.**

R u comin' down? Or am I coming up?

I tap my foot again, and then walk over to the wall mirror to check myself out. I'm borderline raggedy in my sweatpants and baby tee. Plus my hair is everywhere. I could really use a scrunchy right about now.

"You should probably comb your hair if your boyfriend is here," Hope says.

Gia gives her the eye and Hope says, "What? I'm just saying."

I grab a ponytail holder from my dresser and finger comb my thick hair into a high ponytail. If he doesn't like this, then oh well. That's what you get when you visit your angry girlfriend unannounced.

"Do you need me to go downstairs with you?" Gia asks. "Because I will, you know, especially if you think you might need to escape."

"No, I'm good. I do need to talk to him. I wasn't really ready yet, but since he's here, I might as well."

I leave our room, and take the stairs instead of the slow elevator. We're only on the second floor, and waiting for the elevator takes an eternity.

Before he sees me, I spy Sam standing in our lounge next to the door. Dang! Why does he have to look good? I needed to see him looking all scrubbed out, so that I wouldn't want to hug him on sight.

He's got a fresh haircut—his signature low fade, and some new prescription glasses. Are those Prada frames? He must be doing all right up in the NYC. His clothes are on point too. Solid dark red button-down, half tucked, half out, and fitted jeans—not a sag in sight. I see every chick in sight staring him down, probably wondering who he's here to see. He's not giving them any play. I don't even see him make eye contact with anyone.

He better not.

Suddenly, I feel bad that I look a hot booty mess. I spin on one heel to go back into the staircase. I can't let him see me like this!

"Sunday," he calls just as I'm about to make a clean getaway.

I stop in my tracks and hear his footsteps behind me as he walks up. "You change your mind about seeing me?" he asks as he spins me around and pulls me into a hug.

I hug him back. Dang me! The plan was to act hard, but hugging someone tight is soooo the opposite of that. Total fail on my part. I get negative points for my hardness factor.

"I look crazy," I finally say after we're done hugging, but Sam still holds me in his arms. "Let me go upstairs and change."

"Nope. You look awesome. Let's go get something to eat!"

He leans his head in to kiss me, but I turn away. I just

got a mental picture of him tongue twisted with someone else, and it wrecked my flow.

"You don't want to kiss me?" he asks.

"Nope. You already got some lip gloss on you."

Sam reaches up and touches his face. "I do? Where? I thought I got that off!"

He bursts into giggles as I give him a light jab and pull out of his embrace. "Very funny, Sam."

"Okay, okay. I understand. Don't kiss me, right now. You don't have to. But can we go to our spot? I came all the way down here to get some Busy Bee fried chicken. Let's go!"

I put my hands on my hips and poke out my lips. "Seriously? You flew down here to get some fried chicken?"

"Well, I was telling everybody that I was coming to see my girlfriend, my boo, the one I've been missing like crazy, but she just dissed me hard. She ain't even comb her hair when she came downstairs, and she would not let me kiss those pretty lips. . . . So since she ain't missing me back, I want some chicken!"

Dang him! If I could wipe this stupid smile off my face I would!

Instead I shrug. "Okay then. Chicken it is. You driving?"

I hike up my sweatpants and sashay past Sam to the door of our residence hall. Since I'm in so-called diss mode and all that, we can just go get our grub on. He can just keep his tainted lips to himself and buy me some chicken.

"You're treating too, right?" I ask.

Sam bursts into laughter as I stand next to the door.

"You're waiting for me to open the door aren't you? You diss me and then you want me to be a gentleman?"

"Yeah? And?"

Sam smiles, and dutifully opens the door for me. "I guess I deserve this."

"Yep, you kinda do."

Before Sam got here, I didn't really know if we could get past his stupidity with the girl. But now that I see him, and I can tell that he really cares about me, I think maybe I can forget about it all.

Maybe.

As long as he doesn't do any other stupid things.

8

Newcomer Sunday Tolliver continues to impress with each single off her album. "The Highlight" is her first ballad to get radio play and it truly displays her vocal gifts. The song left me with chills, and I don't get chills easily. I'm looking forward to the video, which, I'm told, was filmed at Zillionaire's Atlanta mansion to accommodate Sunday's full-time schedule as a freshman at Spelman. With yet another reality show about to debut, and an album full of single-worthy hits, is there any way Sunday can top her success? Award season is coming up. Expect to see Sunday represented heavily at the AMAs, the Grammys, and the VMAs.

Oh, and by the way, her new single debuted at number one on the Billboard Pop *and* R & B *charts. Sunday Tolliver seems unstoppable.*

"The blogs just love you, don't they?" Piper asks as she finishes reading the Sandra Rose post about me.

I finish folding the last of my laundry and put it in my dresser drawers while I ponder an answer to this question. The blogs do seem to love me—now. But I know that could change in an instant. All I have to do is say one wrong thing to a fan on a bad day, or cross paths with a person who has something to gain by dissing me. It's a scary place to be. Mystique tells me to live in the moment. She says if I worry about what *could* happen, then I'll never enjoy what's actually happening.

"I just take it for what it is," I reply. "Free publicity for the record. The single making it to number one is important to me, because that means ring-tone money and downloads on iTunes and Amazon.com."

Piper stretches out on my bed and continues to play with her phone. "Girl, I wish I had a talent that could make me lots of money. Then, I wouldn't have to worry about all this financial aid and what not. I'm only in school now because my foster parents pulled some strings. I don't know what I'm going to do at the end of the semester."

"What's the problem?"

"Technically, I can't be listed on my financial aid paperwork as an independent adult, because I'm not twenty-three. I have no idea where my mother is to get her to sign off on anything. My foster mom is trying to talk to the financial office to get a waiver for me, but they may not be able to do it by the end of the semester."

"So you might miss half of the year?"

Piper nods. "I should be able to come back next year,

but it would really annoy me if I got behind in my studies just because my mom is holed up in a crack house somewhere."

Long pause, because I have no idea how to respond to this. I couldn't imagine what I'd do or how I'd be if my mom was a drug addict. Piper even being in college is probably incredible. I bet no one thought she'd make it this far.

"Did you talk to them about work study? I think Gia is supposed to be doing that next year."

"I did speak with them about that, but work study is a part of the financial aid program. I can't do any of that until I've got all the forms completed. But I'm not gonna worry about it now. My foster parents paid half of my tuition this semester and got me a scholarship for the other half from Gamma Phi Gamma."

"Maybe you do have a talent that can make money. Your nails always look really good. Do you do them yourself?"

Piper looks down at her set of acrylics. "Yes, I do them myself. I used to charge girls in the foster home, for little designs and stuff. I also do tattoos, but I probably wouldn't be able to do that on campus."

"Um, no to the tats, but yes to the nails! Mostly everyone on campus is half broke. How much would you charge to do a full set?"

"I don't know. Fifteen bucks?"

"If you could do ten people a week that would be a hundred fifty dollars. That's more than you'd make at a fast-food restaurant."

"Probably. That's a good idea. I'm going to get some flyers made. But wait. I don't even have cash to get any equipment. I've barely got enough money to eat off campus."

"I'll buy you the supplies. You can pay me back next year, when you get that first financial aid refund check."

Piper's eyes light up, but then she looks suspicious. "Why would you do that for me?"

"I guess because your situation really sucks and I'm feeling grateful for my mom and my blessings right now. Don't look a gift horse in the mouth, heffa."

Piper laughs out loud. "Okay, I'm just going to say thank you."

"And I'm just going to say you're welcome."

"Guess who I saw at Busy Bee's last night?"

I already know who she saw, because Gia filled me in late last night after they got in. Gia and Ricky were on a "double date" with Kevin and Piper. Well . . . sort of. Kevin didn't realize he was going on a date until he got there, and apparently he wasn't happy. But they saw DeShawn from my video shoot.

"Who did you see, Piper?"

"Gia must've already told you, but we saw DeShawn and he asked about you. He wanted to know if you'd broken up with your boyfriend yet."

To be honest, DeShawn hadn't even come to mind since we shot my video. I was pleased that he asked about me, though. I mean, I am a girl, and he is *ridiculously* gorgeous.

"What did you tell him?" I ask.

"Nothing. I didn't tell him anything. Not even when he gave us tickets to their game in Jacksonville, Alabama."

"He gave us tickets? Are y'all going? When is the game?"

"It's this coming Saturday, and Gia is definitely going. You know she gotta see her little boo play ball and everything."

"How are y'all getting there?" I ask.

Piper grins which lets me know her answer before she speaks a word. "We were hoping you would drive."

I let out a big sigh. "Well, I've got a show on Friday night at The House of Blues. I probably won't feel like driving. Who else has a license?"

"I bet Gia's friend Kevin would drive. He seems really responsible."

"You like him."

"I do, but I'm not sure if I'm his type."

I think back on what Gia said about Kevin and wonder if Piper's crush is a lost cause.

"You think Meagan will want to come too?" I ask changing the subject from Kevin.

Piper scrunches up her nose. "I need a break from her. Plus, I think she likes Kevin too."

I shake my head. "Nope. She's talking to another guy at Morehouse, I think. She hasn't said anything else about Kevin."

"Then, I guess it's okay. I just . . . well . . . she's always reminding me of how privileged she is and how under-privileged I am."

"She does that to all of us, Piper, not just you."

"But the difference between y'all and me, is that y'all really do have something. You're a freaking celebrity. Gia doesn't care about what anyone thinks on anything. I was really hoping that my first roommate would be like a sister to me, but Meagan and I aren't bonding at all."

"Look at it this way. It's only a year, right? Next year, you'll get a new roomie. Maybe we'll all move off campus together."

Why did I let those words fly out of my mouth? That was definitely a thought that should've stayed internal. I don't think I know Piper well enough to live with her. Gia is a no-brainer. She's absolutely gonna be my off-campus roomie, if I can convince her that living in a penthouse is better than shared bathrooms and crummy kitchen space, because when I finally get a check from Epsilon Records (it's supposed to be soon), I'm buying some property.

"You'd want me to live off-campus with you?"

"I mean, unless you've got some secret life I should know about . . ."

Piper jumps off the bed and literally tackles me with a hug. "You really *are* my friend, aren't you?"

Gia walks into our room and shakes her head when she sees us. "Piper, you have got to be the huggingest person I know. Good grief. What did Sunday do? Tell you your hair was cute?"

We all bust our guts laughing at Gia. Then Piper says, "No. She said we're moving off campus with her next year."

"That's what's up!" Gia says. "But did you talk her into driving to the game on Saturday?"

"Halfway. I talked her into going, but she wants Kevin to drive."

"So y'all just scheming on getting my car, huh? Do y'all even want me to go, or do y'all just want the keys?"

Gia and Piper surround me in a hug sandwich. "Of course we want you to go," Gia says. "We loooooove you!"

Looks like I'm going on my first college road trip! Score!

"Look at this mess. Y'all got me hugging folk too!" Gia says.

Sister love! The only thing that would make this picture complete is if Sam was here too. Seeing him for just two days wasn't enough. It's been a week since I've seen him, and already I miss him.

I know that if I want to enjoy kicking it with my friends that I have to put all of that sadness out of my mind. I've got to be strong until the next time I see my boo.

I just hope Sam is missing me as much as I'm missing him.

9

"**S**unday, are you going to let me put these eyelashes on you or not?" Regina, my makeup artist, hovers over me in the cramped House of Blues dressing room looking ready to attack me with a pair of mink eyelashes.

"My vote is no," I reply. "Those things look like caterpillars."

"They'll make your eyes pop when you're on stage."

"Then my eyes shant be popping!" I say. "I'm not getting those things glued on me. Then they'll still be stuck to my eyes tomorrow when I go to the football game. No thank you."

Regina sighs and turns to Mystique for support. "Mystique, will you do something? She's impossible."

"Well, she doesn't *have* to wear them. Do something really dramatic with her eye makeup. Line the bottom and top lids, and put something glittery on top. That should make her eyes pop too."

Regina puts her hands on her hips and scowls at Mystique. She's chewing her gum so hard I think she's gonna break a tooth. I've never seen her this irritated, although I have gotten on her nerves plenty of times with my refusal of all things glam.

"You think I don't know how to make her eyes pop? You want to do the makeup now too, Mystique? Don't you do enough already? Let me do what I do, and you do what you do."

Mystique leans back as if the words are blows. "No one is questioning your skills! I'm just trying to make sure my artist isn't stressed out before her show."

"Am I stressing you out, Sunday? Huh? Am I *really* stressing you out?" Regina asks.

I let out a small chuckle. "You are stressing yourself out, I think. I'm straight as long as you don't try to put those caterpillars on my face."

Regina sighs and gingerly places the mink insects back in their plastic container where they are a safe distance from my eyes.

Mystique talks to me while Regina works on my face. "Sunday, are you sure you want to do your show with a live band? There's still time to do the tracks if you want."

I furrow my eyebrows in a frown and Regina pops me with a makeup brush. "Stop moving!" she fusses.

"Ouch! Mystique, I am a musician and this is a small venue. No background tracks. That's lame."

"Okay, I was just asking. I didn't want you to think you had to do this like you've got something to prove. Everybody knows you can sing."

"I'm not trying to prove anything. I just know that I hate tracks. I hate lip synching and all that."

"So, if you go on tour this summer, you're going to use a live band?"

She asks this question as if there is only one acceptable answer, and not the one I want.

"Well, that's what I thought. Is it not doable?"

"Um . . . well, I don't think Epsilon Records will want to send you on tour with a full band. Maybe if you do some tour stops with me, and I have a full band . . . yeah, maybe that will work."

Regina looks up at Mystique. "You never have a full band. You always sing to a track."

Mystique looks away from Regina's glare. "Yeah, well, I'm an artist too. Sunday isn't the only purist in the music industry."

I don't know what just passed between Mystique and Regina, but there seems to be some hidden conversation in their facial expressions. Mystique seems really uncomfortable all of a sudden.

Mystique says, "I'm going to make sure that everyone in the band is straight, and then I'm going to sit in VIP with Zac and Big D."

"Zac is here?"

"Yep. You're one of his favorite artists right now, honey." She kisses me on the cheek and then wipes off her lip gloss.

Regina is silent for a few moments until Mystique has gotten out of earshot. Then she makes a sound like she's sucking her teeth.

"What's wrong?" I ask.

Regina clears her throat. "Okay, Sunday, I'm gonna tell you something, and you might not believe me now, but you will down the road."

"Okay . . ."

"Mystique is not one hundred percent in your corner. She is not ready to give up that throne, baby, and you are coming hard and strong."

"I-I'm not trying to take her throne."

"You don't have to be *trying*. But it's happening anyway. I heard from a very, very trusted source that she is the one behind that ecstasy getting slipped in Sam's drink."

"Unh-uh! Whatever! I don't believe that."

"My friend who is a makeup artist in Zac's camp said she overheard the girl in the bathroom talking about it. The chic was some random video vixen, and she said Mystique had paid her one thousand dollars to get Sam in a compromising position."

"Yeah, well, if that was true, why hasn't the picture been leaked yet?"

"I haven't figured that part out," Regina says, "but maybe it has something to do with the fact that Sam confessed everything to you. I bet she never expected him to do that."

This is information overload. Too much dang information. This is stuff that Regina should've kept to herself. Mystique is my mentor, for crying out loud. If she didn't want me around, why would she even give me a record deal?

"I owe all of this to Mystique. I wouldn't even have a

gig if it wasn't for her. Shoot, I wouldn't have a record deal if it wasn't for her."

"Yep, and she wants you to never forget that too. Just . . . just watch your back, Sunday. Don't say I didn't warn you about her."

"Okay."

Gia, Piper, and Meagan all storm the backstage with their backstage passes. They're all smiles, which I need right now since Regina just totally wrecked my flow with her overshare.

Regina says, "You're all done. I'm going to watch the show. Knock 'em dead."

"What's wrong?" Gia asks as they crowd my area.

I consider telling them, but I think if I share the story it'll make my mood worse. I need something to get me up.

"Nothing. Just nerves, I guess. Did you guys get good seats?"

Gia nods. "We left Kevin and Ricky out there manning our table. We're front and center. If you get nervous just look at us."

Dilly walks up to us. My friends squeal when he kisses me on my cheek.

"Hey, Sunday. You ready?" Dilly asks.

I shake my head. "Nowhere near."

"And who is this?" Meagan's thirsty self asks.

"He's not a Morehouse man," I reply. "He's a senior in high school."

I laugh out loud as Piper and Meagan immediately lose interest. "Dang, Sunday," Dilly says. "Why you gotta put me on blast all like that?"

"Just wanted to let them know that you're not legal."

Meagan says, "It's too bad, because you're tremendously cute."

"Tremendously," Piper echoes.

"But unfortunately, we can still smell your mama's breast milk on your breath," Gia says.

"Ouch!" Dilly says. "That really, really hurt. Mean girls!"

Piper takes a moment from laughing to say, "We're going to our seats, Sunday. Do good!"

All three of my friends hug me tightly and they leave, but Dilly stays behind.

"Bethany is here," he says somberly.

"With you?"

"Nah, she came with her girls, but she saw me here already."

"Did you talk to her?"

He shakes his head. "No. I told you that I'm done with her. I showed that crazy letter she wrote to my sister and she cussed Bethany out. It's messed up though, because I'm supposed to be on a remix on her record."

"You don't think she'll still want you to do it?"

"Nah, and I don't even want to."

It seems like Dilly and Bethany went up in flames quickly! They were all on each other just a few weeks ago, and now he's running for the hills. Boys!

"You were feeling Bethany something fierce just a minute ago, Dilly. At least you could tell her you've moved on."

"I guess, but you don't need to worry about that right now. You've got a show to do."

"Okay, thanks for coming to check on me."

"Anytime, big sis. When you hear the person out there hollering at the top of their lungs, saying, 'Go, Sunday!' it'll be me."

Now, I'm alone backstage, except for the stagehand girl who keeps giving me time checks. She yelled, "five minutes!" just as Dilly left. If Sam was here, this would be the time when he'd be giving me a pep talk. But I don't even know if he knows about the show.

My cell phone rings. Guess I need to put that on silent before I go on stage. Caller ID says Sam! He does know!

"Hey, Sam."

"Hey, babe, you 'bout to go on stage?"

I shiver when he calls me babe. He says it so casually, like it's actually my name, and he catches me off guard with it every time.

"I am about to go on in about four minutes."

"Well, do good. Make daddy proud."

I laugh out loud. "Really, Sam? Daddy?"

"Was that too much?"

"Way too much."

"Okay, well then make me proud. Your boyfriend who is marooned in the cold butt state of New York."

"Cold? We're still rocking shorts!"

"Exactly, and I need a winter coat right about now. Do you know my car had ice on it this morning?"

I giggle. "I would love to listen to you complain about the weather, because you sound so pitiful doing it, but I really need to go on stage."

"Oh yeah. Call me when you're done."

"Okay. Talk to you later."

"Miss you."

"Miss you more."

I press end to disconnect the call, because if I don't do it, Sam won't and I'll miss my curtain call. It's pretty hard for us to get off the phone since we're so far away from each other.

Sam should be here with me. Especially since I don't know who is in my corner and who isn't. Dreya is always questionable, and Big D has been loyal up until now, but will he be on my side if Mystique turns on me? He's on the come-up for real, and his goal is to make this paper by any means necessary.

How can I survive this whirlwind if I don't know who I can trust?

10

The football game was all that! Georgia State crushed Jacksonville State 28-0, and everyone is celebrating back at the Residence Inn. I know it's not really a four-star, banging hotel for a celebrity type and all that, but I just wanna hang with everybody else.

We got a two-bedroom suite, and we're rolling seven deep in our room. Me, Gia, Hope, and Piper in one bedroom, and Ricky, Kevin, and DeShawn in the other.

We're all chilling in the common area with the television on. My stomach is on growl mode, so I hope we're about to cop some grub. That little bag of popcorn I smashed during the game is not cutting it!

Gia asks, "Ricky, are you and DeShawn sure y'all don't want to be with the team? I would understand if y'all wanted to go with them to that Applebee's. They're just too noisy for me."

"You know I want to be with my girl," Ricky says and kisses Gia's hand sweetly. Awww . . . that's so cute.

Hope giggles from her cross-legged position on the floor. "And you know she wasn't really seriously asking you that question."

"Since I'm trying to get with Sunday, I wouldn't be anywhere else either," DeShawn says. The gleam in his eye is bright and he's smiling hard. I don't smile back, but I feel like I'm blushing something awful.

"I have a boyfriend," I say.

"You keep telling me that, and every time you say it, you sound less and less confident. Sounds like dude needs to get down here and remind you that he exists."

I get ready to respond with a quip of my own, until Kevin makes a noise that sounds like a groan.

"Why does this TV only have like eight channels?" Kevin asks as he squats in front of the TV with the remote clicking frantically. "They don't even have AMC."

"Are you serious?" Hope asks. "Do they have Lifetime?"

"Dude, ain't nobody trying to watch no AMC or Lifetime," DeShawn says with a chuckle.

"Um, *Mad Men* rocks," Kevin replies.

Ricky laughs out loud and asks, "What's on HBO?"

"*No bueno* to HBO. I saw a naked breast when I passed through the first time," Kevin says. "I'm not watching that."

DeShawn smirks, but when no one jumps in to rag on Kevin, he doesn't say anything. I think everyone respects that Kevin is going to go to seminary at Morehouse in addition to his pre-med.

Piper jumps up from the couch and swipes the remote from Kevin. "Does it have BET? Sunday's show is on."

I scrunch my nose. I do not want to watch the show—not with my friends. It's so phony with the little confessionals and all that. Plus we were doing a video shoot in Barbados, so there's quite a bit of footage with me in skimpy swimwear. For some reason I don't want De-Shawn to see that.

DeShawn sits on the floor at my feet and gives me a light punch on the leg. "Yeah, let's watch Sunday's show! I didn't watch the other one."

"My vote is no," I say as I slump back on the couch.

Gia says, "I've already seen this episode. It's a repeat, but it was good! Sunday and Sam help save a girl's life. . . ."

"Well, maybe we want to watch, Gia! Dang!" Ricky says.

Gia's face goes dark and she stares at Ricky. I'm guessing she wasn't digging his tone, because she sure doesn't look happy.

"I mean, babe . . . um . . . can we enjoy the show too?" Ricky asks. Boy, he sure did clean that up quickly.

Gia politely moves from the table where she was sitting next to Ricky and crowds me on the couch.

"You gonna be like that, Gi-Gi?" Ricky asks.

Gia looks at me and grimaces. "I think somebody's head is extra large just because they scored a touchdown tonight. But I think somebody should tell somebody that they can't talk to me any kind of way and think I'm gonna be nice."

"Apologize, Ricky!" Kevin says. "You were kind of harsh."

"Man, she was telling the whole . . ."

Everyone stops and stares at Ricky.

"Never mind," Ricky says. "I'm sorry, Gi-Gi."

"I forgive you." Even though she's extended forgiveness, Gia stays next to me on the couch.

"Are we getting something to eat?" Piper asks. "Who wants pizza and wings?"

"Sounds good," DeShawn says. "What you want, Sunday?"

"I really should have a salad, but I'm feeling like pizza sounds really good right now."

"The show is on!" Piper says as she turns up the volume.

Kevin looks back at me and says, "Sunday, you look really pretty on TV. It doesn't add ten pounds to you at all."

"Maybe five," DeShawn says.

"What?" I say, this time giving him the fake punch. "I beg your pardon!"

"It's okay though. You just look thick. I like my chicks thick."

Gia looks at me and raises an eyebrow, but says nothing. Looks like DeShawn is going to be in flirt mode tonight.

There's a scene with Sam and I playing in the sand and then running to splash in the water. The first time I saw this footage, I thought it was cute. But now, I'm feeling self-conscious about it with DeShawn watching. I wish I had on more of a swimsuit, because he's looking mesmerized.

"That's your dude?" DeShawn asks.

"Yep. That's Sam."

"He doesn't look like your type."

Gia makes a snorting sound. I scowl at her and she straightens up quickly, but Piper is struggling to contain her laughter.

"Oh really? What do you think is my type?" I ask, almost afraid to hear his answer.

"Me. I'm your type."

"I used to date jocks in high school. Didn't really have a good track record with them. Most of them were players."

Piper high-fives in the air from across the room. "Yep, you got that right. I had the same experience with ballers."

Ricky scowls, walks over to the couch, plops down, and puts his arm around Gia. "I disagree with that stereotype. I'm not a player."

"You were in high school," Kevin says. "Remember Valerie?"

"Kevin! Man, whose side are you on?" DeShawn says.

"I remember Valerie," Gia says. "Old juicy booty Hi-Stepper that had your nose open. But that was before us, so that didn't make him a player, Kevy-Kev."

Hope gets up and walks over to the phone. "Ugh. Can we change the subject? I'm gonna order the food."

"I'm trying to watch the show!" Piper fusses.

There's a knock on our hotel room door, and Kevin jumps up to answer it. "The pizza can't be here this fast."

It's Meagan, and she's looking a little bit twisted. "Hey, y'all," she says.

"Hey! What's up, Gamma Junior!" I say. "Where's your girls?"

"They're in the room. Sunday, can I talk to you for just a moment?"

I'm happy to oblige, even though Meagan is irritating, because DeShawn has started rubbing my feet, and somehow I'm thinking that's not going to end well.

"Can we go in the bedroom? I want to ask you something," Meagan says.

"Okay."

I jump up from the couch and out of DeShawn's reach. Meagan follows me into our bedroom and I close the door.

"What's up, girl?" I ask.

"Do you think I can stay in here with y'all?" Meagan asks. "Some of the sorors are tripping a little bit."

"Of course you can stay with us, but what do you mean tripping?"

"They had some marijuana, and I don't use drugs at all. They started smoking and then making fun of me because I didn't want to join in."

"Ugh. Peer pressure is so high school."

"Tell me about it. I'm just tripping about them being Gamma Phi Gammas. I mean, it's just a few of them, but they are definitely not acting in the tradition of this sorority."

"So what are you going to do? Are you still going to hang with them?"

Meagan shrugs. "They're in the sorority, so I don't know how I can really *not* hang with them."

"I don't think you have to. You get in whether they like you or not. Isn't that the most important part? The getting in, I mean."

"No!" Meagan says while shaking her head furiously. "That is not the most important part of being in a sorority. The most important part is the sisterhood. I want them to be my sisters."

"Well, since you're not in Gamma Phi Gamma yet and you can't even join until next year, why don't you just kick it with us? I think we'll make pretty good in-the-meantime sisters."

"I don't mean to diss you guys by being with the Gamma sisters. I hope you don't take it that way."

"Nah, not me. But maybe Piper does."

Meagan rolls her eyes. "Well, Piper gets on my nerves anyway. I don't care what she thinks."

I don't respond to this. If Meagan doesn't like Piper, then they don't have to be friends, but I will not be a part of the drama. Not I, said the fly.

"Well, just come on out and watch TV with us. I won't say anything about Gamma Phi Gamma if you don't," I say.

"Okay."

When Meagan and I emerge from the bedroom, Piper and Gia both stare at us like they want the scoop. I don't sit in my previous seat, because DeShawn is getting out of control. Meagan and I both sit at the kitchen table.

"So, Sunday," Kevin says, "is going to Spelman part of your marketing plan? If so, it's a really good idea. I've never seen a musician use this angle before."

Okay, this dude is about to really get on my nerves. "Ummm, no! Why would I enroll in college to market a record? I've wanted to be an entertainment lawyer for years."

"I'm sorry. I didn't mean to offend you. I just thought it was a good idea."

DeShawn jumps in. "Real talk, though. You're not gonna be able to do this once you really blow up. You're still new, but your record hit number one. It's only a matter of time until you can't go out in public without a bodyguard."

"Keisha Knight Pulliam went to Spelman, and she's just fine," Hope says. "I think Sunday can do it too, if she's really dedicated to it."

Ricky says, "Keisha wasn't at the height of her career. *The Cosby Show* was over. So it's not really the same thing."

"Word! Sunday is just about to become a superstar," Kevin says. Why does slang sound so odd coming from him? It feels like he's trying too hard.

"Listen, y'all," I say, "I do not like discussing my life like I'm some type of social experiment. Right now, I'm a freshman at Spelman with a record deal. That's pretty much it. I don't even have a career yet. I could be a one-hit wonder. So, it is what it is. I'm here, I'm staying, and if you want to be in my circle, get used to it."

Gia chuckles. "*Your* circle? Whatever. This is *our* circle. And if you want to stay in it, you better get used to our opinions. 'Cause I think we're pretty opinionated."

I look at Gia and my jaw drops. Did she just seriously check me? I think she did! Wow . . . I don't know if I should check her back or hug her!

"Are we gonna keep putting Sunday on blast or are we watching TV?" Piper asks.

Gia pats the seat on the couch next to her. "Come on, sister. We're not done discussing your swim attire."

I abandon Meagan at the table and plop down next to Gia, feeling incredibly normal. It's a feeling that I like, and one that I'm going to cherish. Just in case things get crazy . . . I plan to remember this moment.

My phone buzzes and I look down to see a message from Mystique. Just got top-secret AMA nomination list. Get ready to shine, baby girl.

I know this should make me happy! I should get up and do some kind of happy dance. But after the conversation we just had, getting this text makes me feel like my normal days are numbered, and Sunday Tolliver, college freshman, is about to be eclipsed by Sunday Tolliver, pop star.

I think one day I'll have to choose. I'm glad it's not today.

11

"How do you feel, baby?" My mom called me as soon as the American Music Awards nominations were announced.

"Um . . . excited, I guess. It feels weird though. I remember getting up early to hear the nominees announced. So it's kind of crazy being on the list."

"Just try to breathe and take it easy. Have you talked to Sam?"

"Not yet. I'm sure he'll be calling me in a minute. I'm going to hide out over at Zac's house for lunch with Mystique, and I'll probably spend the night."

"That doesn't sound like much of a hideout. Why don't you come home and spend the night?"

I think about this for a second, and I almost say yes, but I'm not trying to kick it with Aunt Charlie and Manny. Aunt Charlie has this new thing where she hits me up for money every time we're in the same room. That ain't cool at all.

"I'll come home soon, but I think Mystique also wants to talk about some business stuff too."

"Okay, honey. Call me later, so we can go out and celebrate your nomination."

"Okay, Mom."

I press end on the phone and look up at Gia. She does a little fashion-model spin, so I guess she wants me to say something about her outfit. She's wearing a knee-length jean skirt, gladiator sandals, and an orange sweater vest with a baby tee underneath. It's still hot outside, but technically it's fall. She's got a summer-meets-fall vibe going on.

"You look cute."

"Thanks. It's an experiment."

"An experiment in what?"

"Girly-girl clothes. Skirts are not really my apparel item of choice, but I want to try and give them a chance."

I chuckle. Gia takes everything so seriously. I mean, for real, it's just an outfit.

"Where are you and your experiment going today?"

"Went to class already, and now I'm about to go job hunting. I did the whole online application thing, but I think some of these places need to see me in my fabulous glory. Then they'll hire me on the spot."

"I've got a job for you, if you'll take it."

"What does it pay?"

"Four hundred dollars, plus fifty bucks for every rehearsal."

Gia scrunches her eyebrows together. "Tell me more . . ."

"Mystique told me that I've been invited to perform at the American Music Awards, and I want you and Ricky to lead the backup dancers. What do you think?"

Gia comes running toward me like a freight train with her arms outstretched. Hugging time. I guess that's a yes, then.

"This is going to be so incredible," Gia gushes. "I need the music, like immediately."

"Yes, I'll have it for you this week. How long do you think it will take you to choreograph something?"

"Is it fast or slow?"

"Does that make a difference?"

"Yeah. I'm better at fast songs, but I can do both."

"More than likely it'll be fast, but I meet with Mystique today. I'll know for sure tomorrow."

"Cool. So your cousin got nominated too?"

"Yeah, it's tripped out. Dreya, Truth, and I are all nominated for the T-Mobile Breakthrough Artist. Sam and I are also nominated for Song of the Year, because we wrote Mystique's hit record."

"Y'all wrote that?"

"Yep. That's what got Mystique interested in me. It's the reason she gave me a record deal."

"Ricky and I are definitely up for the choreography job. Is it okay that I don't have any formal dance training?"

"Nobody trained me to be a singer or a songwriter. Some things you're born with, I guess."

Gia gathers a stack of papers from her desk. "After I get done with the job search, I'm going to study with

Piper. We've got a science test on Friday. How'd you do on your essay for Composition?"

"I did okay, got a B, but if I'd had more time, I know I could've gotten an A."

"Hmmm . . . well, let me know when you get back from Zac's house, so I can know what I'm working with."

"Okay."

Gia hugs me again (enough with the hugs!) and walks out of our room with those gladiator sandals clicking the tiled floor. I didn't miss her pause when I told her my grade. I know she got an A on her paper. I should've too. Would've, had it not been for a late-night session with Bethany. She couldn't get the bridge right on one of her songs, and Big D called me for an emergency session. I ended up turning in the first draft of my paper. It had typos and everything. The only thing that saved me was that it was well thought out, and I'd done my research.

But I was not satisfied with the B. I won't get into a good law school with B's. I need to pull all A's in my courses. Have to.

I don't want to end up one of these artists who have a few hits and make a few dollars, and then you hear about them five years later, losing their houses and cars, and starring on jacked-up reality shows. That's not going to be me or Sam.

I drive to Zac's house with all of this on my mind, and the stuff that Regina told me about Mystique. It had a ring of truth to it, especially the part about Mystique not being ready to give up her throne. But with her eight American Music Award nominations, she's clearly still the queen and all the other people in the music industry are her subjects.

There are lots of cars in Zac's driveway as I pull in. I thought this was a meeting, but it looks more like a party. It sounds like a party too. I can hear the music from the street. I wish I'd just stayed at the dorm and studied if we're not having a conference.

Mystique's bodyguard, Benji, meets me at my car and opens the door. His long wavy hair is hanging loose, but his tailored suit lets me know that he's all business.

"Sunday! It took you long enough, princess. The party is under way."

"I thought this was a meeting."

"Yeah, y'all are meeting in Zac's boardroom in about an hour. Some of the Epsilon executives are here from New York."

They flew in from New York City? This must be an important meeting then. What could this be about? Not to mention that I'm totally underdressed in my jeans, baby tee, and flip-flops—my campus uniform.

I follow Benji into the house and he walks me to Zac's VIP lounge. It's tripped-out when you have so many guests that you have to have a VIP section in your house.

A big grin spreads across my face when I see Sam leaned back on the couch smiling from ear to ear. I should've known he'd be here if people were flying in from New York.

He jumps up and hugs me. I give him a playful poke in the stomach (which is rock hard, by the way. He's been working out).

"Why didn't you tell me you were coming?" I ask.

"I wanted to surprise you. Are you surprised?"

I nod. "Congratulations, Songwriter of the Year."

He tosses his head back and laughs. "Wouldn't that be sick if we win?"

"OMG! It would be ridiculous if we win."

Mystique comes in the room. She's wearing a new weave. It's blonde and pin straight and it comes to her waist in the back, but it's layered in the front. The whole look is finished off with a feathery bang. She's wearing a one-piece shorts set that barely covers her entire booty. Her long legs look even longer with her four-inch heels.

She looks downright intimidating. And I think that was the plan.

Mystique glides (yes, glides) over to me and air kisses me. She'd have to bend down to actually kiss my face because with the heels she towers over me.

"Congratulations on your nominations," I say.

"You too, sweetie. The heads of Epsilon Records are so proud of you."

Sam leads me over to the couch as Mystique goes to join Zac at the bar.

"Did you see Drama when you got here?" he asks.

I roll my eyes. Not in the mood for Dreya today. "No. She's here? Is Bethany here too?"

"Yes, unfortunately for Dilly, she's here."

I chuckle. "He told you about them? Where's he?"

"Probably somewhere hiding from Bethany. He told me she was basically stalking him."

"Yeah, pretty much. He tried to break up with her, but he doesn't think it worked."

I hope Bethany finds another guy to obsess over soon.

That's all it will take, really, for her to get over Dilly. She's not really the type to chase down a guy who doesn't want her. He's got to be showing some interest.

Dilly walks into the room wearing his jeans and his signature button-down shirt and sweater. That's his thing now. He calls it "pretty nerd swag". I think it's crazy, but rappers have to have something that sets them apart.

He's let his hair grow in thicker, and his sideburns and edges are lined up to perfection. The contrast of his dark hair and sun-kissed light skin are very hot. I see why he's not checking for Bethany anymore. He could have his choice of girls.

He leans over to hug me and kiss my cheek. "Hey, Sunday! Congrats!"

"Thank you, Dilly! You look hot! If I wasn't with Sam . . ."

"But she *is* with me," Sam interjects, "so don't even think about it."

Dilly laughs out loud. "All right, big dog! I remember what you did to Truth. Trust, I don't want none of that. But I did ask Sunday to be my prom date if I don't have anyone else to go with."

Sam frowns. "Nah, chief. You gonna have to find yourself a young cutie. You should be able to after your single comes out."

My eyes light up! "You're finally getting a single out there? Get the heck outta here! Why didn't you tell me?"

"I was going to! I just wanted to do it in person, and you act like you can't come up for air once you start hitting those books."

I shake my head. "I haven't been hitting them hard

enough. I got a B that should've been an A. I shouldn't even be here right now. I need to be back in my room studying. I've got some reading to finish for my history class."

"See, that's why I went ahead and dropped my classes for this semester," Sam says. "There's too much work to be done, and this is my time to strike. I can go to school when I'm rich."

My mouth flies open and my eyes widen to capacity. I can't believe what I'm hearing. Sam dropped out of school? Why didn't he tell me this before now?

"Are you back in Atlanta then?" Dilly asks.

"Nah, I'm still in New York. Zac wants me there more than here, so I'm keeping my apartment there. Zac says I can just crash here when I'm in Atlanta."

Big D walks into the VIP area with Dreya on his arm. Somebody told *them* there was going to be a party. Dreya has on a black shorts jumpsuit that's sheer at the top, and she's wearing a red lace bra underneath. Her red heels look like they hurt, but they are no doubt the business. She's got in a new weave too, but hers is a gigantic, red curly afro that's pinned up on the sides. Her fire-engine-red lipstick is exactly the same shade as the hair.

She is dressed to impress. I feel like I need to go and change.

"Hey, Sunday. I would congratulate you on your nomination, but since we're competing for the same award, I'm just gonna say good luck."

I smile. "Well, I'm gonna be gracious and congratulate you, cousin. May the best chick win."

Dreya laughs out loud. "All right, Sunday. I see you."

Big D gives Sam a fist bump that turns into a hug and he kisses me on the cheek. "Y'all both are a sight for sore eyes. Sunday, you been ghost for a few days. We been missing you down at the studio."

I scrunch my eyebrows together. "I was just there a couple of nights ago."

"It's getting to be that we could use you there every day. Your touch is on just about everyone's album coming out of this camp."

"It is, but I've got school, so I can't be there every day. You know that, D!"

Big D gives me a look that I can't decipher. It's a mixture of puzzlement and irritation.

"You are still cool with me being in college, right? Seems like everybody is tripping on me being at Spelman all of a sudden."

"Nah, I ain't tripping," Big D says. "But everybody's money is riding on you."

Mystique interjects, as she air kisses Big D. "Everyone's money is not riding on Sunday, Darius. We talked about this. Epsilon likes the fact that she's in school. It's positive publicity for the label."

Bethany comes into the VIP suite, and she looks totally different from the last time I saw her. She looks like she's aged five years. Her long hair is flat-ironed pin straight, and she's got a tattoo of some pattern going all the way down her arm to her hand. She's also lost weight—at least twenty pounds. That badonkadonk she used to have has totally disappeared.

"Hey, everybody. Congratulations, everybody," she says before sliding onto one of the couches. She seems totally out of it as she stares at Dilly. He fidgets uncomfortably, but doesn't make an effort to go anywhere near Bethany.

Zac's assistant comes into the VIP suite and announces, "The Epsilon executives are ready to meet now."

We all file out of the room as if we're on our way to see the President of the United States or something. I wonder if it's going to be a good meeting. If the smile plastered on Mystique's face is any indicator, I'm thinking we should be straight.

There are two men and a woman already seated at the boardroom table when we walk in. I notice that the black guy with the crisp gray suit, pink tie, and huge diamond-encrusted watch is sitting at the head of the table. The power seat.

Neither man stands up from the table as we enter, and I don't care who they are, I think this is pretty rude. They must've been raised up north, because no Southern man would stay seated when women enter the room.

"Look at Epsilon's rising stars!" the guy with the diamond watch says. "Y'all so bright, I should've worn my Chanel shades. UV rays popping off y'all like crazy."

Zac says as everyone sits, "Allow me to introduce y'all to Evan Wilborn, Caterina Schmidt, and Lawrence Cohen, the heads of Epsilon Records. They already know who you are."

Evan, the one wearing all the bling, says, "Yes, we know, and congratulations on your success thus far. Big D, you and Mystique have accomplished some wonderful things with this crew, almost by accident."

"Completely by accident," Lawrence says. "We've hardly put any marketing behind these projects and still they manage to get number ones. We have no doubt that Dilly's single featuring Drama, and Drama's single featuring Dilly, will reach the same status."

Caterina nods, but says nothing. She doesn't have to, because Evan seems to like the sound of his voice.

He continues, "Now, it's time to put our money where our mouths are at Epsilon Records. We're putting the marketing machine, and the money behind each of these projects. I want this crew to come out in force and take over the rap game, the R & B game and the pop game. We've got all the talent we need in this room, and you're all so young."

"You've got plenty of time to reign supreme," Caterina says.

Lawrence says, "Getting straight to the point, we're going to combine all of your efforts. Big D in the A Records, Mystical Sounds and Zillionaire Records will be combined under one huge conglomerate called Reign Records. You will be the kings and queens of the industry."

Big D says, "I didn't know that I put Big D in the A Records up for sale. I've never been a part of Epsilon. I've discovered some great artists that you've compensated me handsomely for, but I am an independent."

"And what exactly have you accomplished as an independent?" Evan asks. "You were barely afloat until Sunday came along. And then who did you have? Truth? He was a headache from day one. Talented but troubled, and everybody knew it. Not one major label wanted to fool with him."

"Truth just needs some guidance," Big D says. "He's one of the best rappers in the industry right now."

"But he'll never have any longevity," Caterina says. "Not with his history of violence."

"We're talking about making Reign Records a force to be reckoned with," Lawrence says. "We've already got major endorsements lined up. A movie deal in the works for Sunday. Television appearances for Drama. This is the beginning of a hostile takeover of the industry."

Somehow, I feel like we're being suckered and bamboozled, like there's something they're not saying. Everything sounds good. Too good.

"Why do you want to do this for us?" I ask. "I mean, you can find any talented artists, and put money behind them and make them blow up. It just takes some hot songs and some intense marketing."

"I'm glad you asked that," Evan says. "We're about creating a legacy. We could find any artists and make millions, but your talent—especially you, Sunday—is unique. This could mean a legacy for all of us. Not just a financial legacy, but an artistic one. Do you understand what I mean by that, Sunday?"

"Yes, I do. You want to leave something behind for the next generation."

Evan nods and smiles. "Exactly! I want them to sample our music. I want Epsilon Records to be the success that everyone wants to duplicate. We can do it, you know. With just the people in the room, we can change the game."

"We're game changers," Mystique says. "We've already changed the game. Never have there been three Epsilon Records artists vying for T-Mobile Breakthrough Artist. Everyone is watching to see what will happen with us."

"Does the person who wins get some extra shine? How's that going to work?" Dreya asks.

"You've got to stop thinking about just yourself," Evan says. "Don't you see that whichever of you wins, it is a win for Reign Records? Shoot, you all go on stage together and accept the award."

"As a matter of fact," Mystique says, "for every award that anyone from our camp wins, we all go on stage. Every one of us. We make a statement at the AMAs. We are a family, and there's no competition here."

I find it funny to hear Mystique give this speech, after what Regina told me. But who knows? Maybe Regina was wrong, and maybe Mystique is drinking the Reign Records Kool-Aid. I don't care what label we're on, as long as they keep signing my checks. That's the most important part for me. I can't finish school if the money stops rolling in.

Sam speaks up, "So will I be producing on every Reign Records album?"

"You'll be one of the executive producers for these albums, along with Mystique and Sunday on their individual records and with Big D and Zac on everyone else's," Evan says.

"This all sounds like a dream come true," Bethany says. "Where do I sign? Let's get this party started!"

Evan jumps up and hands Bethany a jewelry box. "That's what I'm talking about, honey. I love your enthusiasm."

Bethany stares down at the box in her hand. "Go ahead and open it," Evan says.

Inside the box is a beautiful diamond pendant with a crown on it. Evan takes it from Bethany's hands and clasps it around her neck.

"This crown is the Reign Records trademark," Caterina says. "We've had one custom made for each of you."

How did they know we'd say yes?

"Is everybody down?" Zac asks. "Does anyone have any objections?"

"I can't sign anything without my sister being here," Dilly says, "but I have absolutely no objections, whatsoever."

Evan says, "We're taking over BET for spring break. All of their programming will be about us. Every show will be hosted by us. Either on location at the beach or from a studio in Atlanta or New York."

"I have a question," I ask. "How is this hostile takeover of the industry going to affect me and my education? I'm serious about becoming an entertainment lawyer. It's what I plan to fall back on when all of this is over."

"Don't you see, Sunday?" Evan says. "If we do this correctly, you will never be broke again. Never, sweetie. You'll be buried in a platinum casket if you want. Game changers don't have to worry about day jobs."

"That all sounds good, but it's still a theory for now," I say. "I believe in everything we're planning to do, but I have to work around my school schedule. That's the only way I can be on board."

Evan looks exasperated. Guess what? I don't care.

"Okay, Sunday, I understand where you're coming

from, but can we reevaluate this at the end of your freshman year? If we are successful enough, you can always revisit your law degree," Lawrence says.

"The only way I'm signing anything is if we understand how important college is to me," I repeat stubbornly.

"All right, Sunday," Evan says. "Your contracts will stipulate that we must work around your school schedule. It will mirror the contract you signed with Mystical Sounds."

"That's what I'm talking about," I reply, feeling like I've won a battle, but that this is just the beginning of a war.

Evan hands me a jewelry box. "With this chain, I thee wed."

"Reign Records, baby!" I say.

"We reign supreme in this mutha!" Dreya says, "I don't need stipulations. Just show me the dotted line. Sunday on that school stuff, I'm on this get-my-money stuff."

You dang skippy, I'm about this school stuff. I'm not dropping out of school for anyone. Too many doors opened up for me to be able to attend school. Everything fell into place with the music, giving me just enough money to enroll without student loans. There's no way I can ignore that. My mother would say that I was meant to have my education.

I would agree with her.

12

"Sam, I can't believe you just dropped out of school like that."

Sam sighs as he packs our suitcases into the trunk of my car. Me, Gia, Ricky, and Sam are going on a double date for the weekend in Destin. We've just finished our first exams and it's time for our fall break. It's just a long weekend, but we need it so badly.

We're going to spend part of the weekend playing and part working. Gia and Ricky are going to teach me the choreography they've done for my American Music Awards performance. We're doing a medley of "Can U See Me" and a dance remix of "The Highlight." Piper wanted to tag along, but I nixed it. I don't want her to feel like a fifth wheel.

"Sunday, it's four o'clock in the morning. Way too early for your fussing."

"Would you rather I fuss now or when we get to the

beach? Because when I get to the beach, I want to walk on the sand and play in the water, know what I mean?"

"I know what you mean."

"So tell me, why did you drop out? And why didn't you say anything to me about it until we were at Zac's house?"

"I dropped out because I'm not like you, Sunday. I'm not an overachiever. I can't do both."

"You didn't even try, Sam. You gave up too easily."

"What am I giving up? Doing music is my dream, Sunday. Reign Records is my dream come true. Don't ruin this for me. Oh, and by the way, I didn't tell you because you're not my mother or my wife."

"Speaking of your mom, what did she say about you dropping out of school?" I just know that Sam's mom was disappointed.

"Unlike you, she thought it was great. She didn't want me to wear myself out going to school and working for Epsilon. She fully supports this."

Now this quiets me down really quickly. I don't know what else I can say to get Sam to go back to school. I just don't want Sam to get all wrapped up in Evan's fairy tale.

After the meeting at Zac's house, I Googled Evan. Did my research. He was an independent label owner when he started. Something like Big D, but he was out of Philadelphia. He had a whole stable of artists, primarily rappers, but some singers and models (okay, models is a stretch. They were video vixens/groupies/tramps). Anyway, after Evan got his name on the map with a female rapper named The Essence, you never heard from anyone in his camp again. Even The Essence crashed and burned after two records. She ended up on drugs and eventually no one wanted to work with her. Evan thrived, though. He made such an impression on the industry with his brand of one (himself) that Epsilon invited him to be a vice president at their company. Now, five years later, he's a partner.

The thing that stuck with me was the disappearance of his artists. They all, more or less, ended up being one-hit wonders. I don't want that to happen to us. We're too talented to get lost in the matrix.

"All right, Sam, I hear you. I understand, and I won't say anything else about it, but don't hurt me by saying my opinion doesn't matter. Your opinion matters to me."

Sam's face softens immediately. "I didn't mean it that way. Of course your opinion matters. That's why I'm so upset that you disagree. If I didn't care what you think, I wouldn't be angry. Can we just celebrate our AMA nominations on the beach and work out these dance moves?"

"Yes, we can."

Sam's smiling at me now, which makes me feel good. I know he's not angry at me, and I don't want him to be, since he's going back to New York City on Tuesday morning.

Gia and Ricky walk up with their little overnight bags, and Sam puts those in the trunk. Gia is ready for the beach! She's got a swimsuit top on with her shorts. The weather is cooling off. It's only in the upper seventies today, but it's still warm enough for a beach weekend, and it'll be a little warmer in Destin.

"We've got a mutiny on our hands," Gia says.

"What mutiny?"

"Piper, DeShawn, Kevin, and Meagan have a car. They got it from one of Meagan's future sorors. And they said they're crashing our trip!"

I laugh out loud. "Well, okay, I guess. Is Piper trying to stay in our room?"

"Piper and Meagan. DeShawn and Kevin are determined to stay with the guys."

Sam says, "See, it wouldn't be like this if the rooming arrangements were how I wanted them to be."

I lift an eyebrow at Sam and shake my head. Lately, he's been hinting that he wants to hook up, and I've been pretty successful at refusing. I care about Sam a whole lot, but what if we sleep together and then we break up? I will feel like it was a waste.

"Gia and Ricky didn't want to do couples rooms either."

Sam rolls his eyes. "Right. I've landed with the purity bunch."

"Nothing wrong with it, man!" Ricky says. "What's the rush? You've got your whole life for all that."

"We're taking you to church next time you come to Atlanta," Gia says. "You need some Jesus Christ in your life."

"What? I go to church!" Sam says. "Y'all tripping."

Ricky says, "Naw, I feel your pain, bro. I feel your pain."

We all pile into the car, but just before we pull off, the carful of party crashers drives up next to us. Kevin is at the wheel, DeShawn is riding shotgun, and the girls are in the back.

Kevin rolls down his window. "Is it cool for us to tag along? You guys aren't angry, are you?"

Gia rolls down her back window. "No, we're not angry, but y'all still some busters!"

Everyone bursts into laughter, including Sam, who spent the last few minutes brooding over his lack of getting any. He might as well get that off the brain, because it's not going down.

Sam says to Kevin, "Do you need to follow me or do you know the way?"

"We've got a GPS, but can we try to stay together? Just for safety?"

Sam nods. "Yep, but don't drive too slowly. I get my roll on, nahmean?"

"I observe all of the traffic laws," Kevin says. "Are you going to be speeding?"

I shake my head at Sam to keep him from responding. Sam just nods as I roll the window up.

Then he says, "I suppose we'll get there tomorrow."

"Destin is like six hours away," Gia says.

"Not with grandpa driving behind us."

I feel myself getting drowsy as soon as the car starts rolling. The GPS navigator is charged up and perched on the dashboard. I get into my comfortable position and fluff up my pillow.

Sam laughs. "I should've put you in the back with Gia. I need some conversation, and I can see right now you plan on going to sleep."

"Okay, we can switch."

I climb over the back seat, dragging my pillow and blanket with me. Ricky then climbs over me and into the front seat. His move wasn't as graceful as mine, but it's done.

Gia's phone rings. "Hello? . . . Oh hush! . . . Well, so is talking on the cell phone while driving."

Gia presses end on her touch screen with a huff. "That was Kevin," she says. "He said to tell y'all that climbing over seats is not safe."

"Boo to Kevin! I'm going to sleep now. Wake me up when we get to the beach."

I actually wake up on my own when the scent of the ocean breeze floats through the open windows.

"Are we there yet?" I ask while stretching as much as I can in the back seat of the car.

"About fifteen minutes away from the hotel, according to the GPS," Ricky replies.

I look out of the back window and see Kevin following close behind. DeShawn sees me turn around and he waves at me. Okay, what was I thinking saying that they could come along—especially DeShawn and all of his flirtatiousness?

"So Ricky tells me that DeShawn was in your video for 'The Highlight,'" Sam says. "How did that go? Was he cool?"

My eyes widen as I bite my lower lip. Is Sam reading my mind or something? Have I put out any clues to let him think I might even be remotely interested in De-Shawn? Because I'm not, even though he's interested in me.

"DeShawn is cool, but I think he's hanging with us because he plays ball with Ricky. He does the modeling gig on the side."

Sam grins at me in the rearview mirror. "You okay, Sunday? You sound a little skittish."

"Why would you be interrogating me when I first wake up?"

"I didn't know I was interrogating you."

Ricky says, "We were talking about the video shoot right before you woke up, Sunday. No biggie. I was just telling Sam how pumped me and Gia are to get to dance on stage on national TV. That's gonna be something great to put on my resume."

"They're talking about doing a spring break tour. You think y'all would want to dance for that too, if I can make it happen?" I ask.

"Of course I would! Gia's still asleep, but I'm sure I can speak for her too when I say yes!"

We pull up to the Sandestin Resort. This place is off the chain, and I got Epsilon Records to pay for the suites when I told them we were coordinating the American Music Awards performance.

Sam and I walk inside to the front desk to check in while the rest of the boys load our luggage on two carts. The weather is warm and muggy, so the cool air-conditioning in the front lobby is welcomed.

When we're done checking in and getting the room keys, I turn around and see Dreya strutting through the lobby wearing a cute sundress. She's ditched her red wig for a wet and wavy sew-in weave, which at the current time is wet. Her two new sidekicks, Tasia and Kiki, are with her, and they both have on swim apparel too. Kiki's got on a bikini top with some board shorts and flip-flops. Tasia's long legs and big booty are on full display in a tiny miniskirt that almost, but not quite covers her cakes. Her swim top is about two sizes too small, so she looks like she could have a wardrobe malfunction at any moment.

"Sunday!" Dreya says as she trots toward me with arms outstretched. A hug? Really?

"What took y'all so long to get here?" Dreya asks. "We've been here since yesterday."

"We weren't planning to be here until today. Did Big D tell you we'd be here yesterday?"

"No . . . Evan flew us in. He said that Reign Records artists should show up together all over the place, but keep it classy at all times."

Tasia is giving Sam the eye like I'm not even here. Rude heifer will get smacked with a quickness if she keeps that up. Kiki plays with her phone and seems oblivious to the fact that we're here.

"Hi, Kiki. Hi, Tasia," I say with a polite wave.

Tasia's face lights up and she runs over to hug me too. I'm sure the man who walked behind her while she hugged me got a great view of her hind parts.

"I can't believe you remember my name!" Tasia says. "I didn't expect you to."

"Why wouldn't I? You're friends of my cousin, so of course I would."

Kiki looks up and gives us a head nod, and then goes back to her phone. I guess that was a hello.

I do not understand how Kiki and Tasia equal "keeping it classy," but whatever. "We're going to work on some choreography for the awards show."

"I know," Dreya says. "Evan told me to get with you about that too, because he wants me to rap on your song.

He wants everyone to know that there's no beef, and it's all love with the Reign artists."

Okay, I wasn't irritated at first, but now I am super annoyed. The smug look on Dreya's face tells me that she thinks she has an ally in Evan. It's not like I don't want her to have anyone on her team, but it was sure a lot easier when she wasn't constantly showing up, already in the know.

"All right, let us get settled in first and we'll call you when we're ready to work."

Dreya nods. "We're on our way to the beach. Maybe we'll see you out there."

Sam and I watch the hood-like trio walk away as do the majority of the guests here at the Sandestin. I don't think they're used to seeing this type of activity in their quiet little five-star resort. I just pray that Dreya doesn't give anyone a reason to treat her badly.

"What's up with that?" Sam asks. "Why didn't you know she was coming? Can somebody spell blindsided?"

I don't answer Sam's questions because I'm dialing Mystique. Because of what Regina told me, I don't trust Mystique enough to tell her what I think of Evan. I will keep that to myself, but I do want to get her opinion of Dreya being a part of my performance at the American Music Awards.

"Hey, Sunday. Did you make it to Destin?" Mystique asks.

"I did. Guess who else is here?"

"I know, Drama. Evan told me he wanted her there. Are you cool with that?"

"I'm cool if you are. I just wanted to get your take on the whole thing."

Mystique sighs deeply. "Honestly, I don't really like it. I've been working really hard to separate your brand from Drama, but Evan insists on putting you back together on stage. He thinks it'll be good for Epsilon Records as a whole."

"Have you shared your concerns?"

She chuckles. "You don't *share* your concerns with Evan. You do what he says. I'm a pretty big star for Epsilon, and I can throw my weight around a little bit, but at the end of the day, I have a contract and albums to fulfill. It seemed like they were giving me some freedom with Mystical Sounds, but now they're taking it all back."

"That's kind of messed up. . . ."

"Yeah, it's real messed up, but they're the money behind the operation. There's really nothing I can do. Zac and Evan are good friends too, so I'm kind of stuck here."

"So that means I'm stuck with Dreya on stage with me at the performance."

"Yes, but not those skanks she's taken to hanging out with. They are not Epsilon artists, and the vixen chick just looks like she stinks. No thank you."

"All right. I'll call you back later and let you know how it goes. Dreya's acting pretty normal, which is actually kind of crazy for her."

"Okay. You can handle it. A real star shines in every situation. Drama can't take anything away from you."

"Thanks, Mystique. Talk to you later."

I end the call feeling less optimistic about Evan than I did before. I wonder why he's taking a liking to Dreya. It's probably because I asked too many questions and she doesn't make it a secret that we're not the best of friends. Maybe it's his way of getting the scoop on what my camp is doing.

I turn on the smile when I get back outside with the crew. I don't want them to think that something is up, because even though Dreya is here, we're still going to enjoy this weekend.

DeShawn is talking to Sam, which makes me a little nervous, but they seem to be hitting it off. Sam's arms are waving wildly as he talks, which lets me know he's talking about music. DeShawn is listening intently. So far so good. As long as DeShawn doesn't flirt with me, we should have a fun time.

Kevin starts pulling the luggage-laden cart toward the door. "Excuse me! A little help here!"

Sam rushes to help Kevin pull the cart inside. DeShawn takes this opportunity to whisper in my ear. "Don't worry, I won't tell Sam about us."

A little growl escapes my throat. Who does DeShawn think he is? I mean, yes, he is ridiculously fine, and yes . . . he has a muscle-bound body to boot, but he doesn't have anything on Sam.

DeShawn chuckles and jogs ahead to help the guys with the bags. Gia links arms with me while Meagan and Piper follow closely behind.

"What are you going to do about DeShawn?" Gia asks. "He's bold as what!"

Piper says, "Yeah, he kept talking about how he was gonna get you to break up with Sam."

I shake my head. "I'm not gonna do anything about him. I wish he wasn't here, but I guess he's cool with Kevin and Ricky."

Meagan says, "I don't see what's so wrong with giving him some play. Didn't you just get mad at Sam for tongue kissing some skank at the club? Looks like he's having his fun."

"I believe what Sam told me about being drugged," I say. "Why would he even tell me if he was up to no good?"

"Maybe he thought you'd find out anyway and that it was inevitable," Meagan says.

"Now you sound like my pessimistic cousin, Dreya, who's here by the way."

Gia crinkles her nose. "Drama is here? Why?"

"She's performing with us at the AMAs. So, I'm stuck with her, according to the record company."

"Well, I hope she doesn't start any mess," Piper says. "I want to have fun this weekend and not end up on the Internet."

"Tell me about it," I say.

Not starting anything would be completely unlike Dreya, but maybe she's ready for a change in her world too. She's not really getting anywhere with her funky attitude and gangsta antics. This could be the opportunity for a wonderful change.

Yeah . . . well . . . I can wish, can't I?

13

"So here are the moves. . . . They're really simple, but the slickness of it is to keep your upper body completely still while you move your feet, legs, and knees."

Gia must see the look of sheer confusion on my face, because she continues, "Just watch me and Ricky, and then you'll see what I mean."

Ricky uses the remote control to turn on the music. When the music blares from the speakers, they slide across the conference room floor with ease, like they're not even thinking of the next move. They both have serious facial expressions, but when they get to the chorus, both their faces light up with smiles. So, the somber faces must've been intentional.

When the music ends, Dreya laughs out loud and says, "Girl, bye! I don't know who you think is about to do all of that. I am not doing all that sliding and jumping and dropping on my knees."

"I want to try to learn," I say, "but I'm nowhere near as talented as you guys. This is going to take a miracle."

Gia pulls me onto the floor. "Not a miracle, but a lot of practice."

"Does anyone else want to learn?" I ask. "Here's your chance to be on the American Music Awards."

Both Meagan and Kevin shake their heads no, but Piper jumps up. "I thought you'd never ask," she says.

"Can you dance?" Ricky asks.

"I'm gonna ignore that obviously racially motivated comment! Of course I can dance. Do you think I'd make a fool out of myself in front of you meanies?"

Kiki and Tasia stand up too, even though I wasn't really talking to them. They're part of Dreya's entourage anyway, so if she's not gonna learn the dance, why are they trying to learn it? DeShawn decides to join us as well.

When everyone in the room is standing in two straight lines, Dreya stomps over. "I will try, but if I don't get it quick, then I'm done."

Kevin stands up, and says, "Meagan and I are going to the beach. We'll see y'all at dinnertime."

Ricky and Gia exchange surprised glances that melt into smiles. I wonder what they're thinking. I've noticed Kevin and Meagan hitting it off on more than one occasion, and he's her type too.

I look over my shoulder at Piper, and she's frowning, but Kevin made it clear that he wasn't trying to get at her. I don't think she wanted to admit that, but it's the truth.

"Okay, everybody. This should be simple because it's basically five moves, and then we do variations of them on each turn. So the first is stomp, stomp, kick, cross, stomp. We'll start off slowly."

After a few tries, everyone gets the first move, except Dreya. But she's not trying very hard.

"We're not going to go on until Drama gets it," Gia says. "Everyone, take five except me, Ricky, and Drama."

They work with her for another fifteen minutes, and she gets it. Finally. But we've got four more moves to go.

By the time we learn the entire routine, it's three hours later and we are drenched in sweat. Kevin and Meagan finally rejoin us, both looking as if they've had a wonderful time.

"Kevin, can you record us doing this step?" I ask. "We're going to give everyone copies of it so we can practice."

"Who's got the camera?"

I point to my bag that's sitting on the chair. Meagan rushes to get the camera for Kevin, and then he smiles appreciatively when she hands it to him.

"Thank you, Meagan."

"You're welcome, Kevin."

Gia looks at me and we hurry to start the dance, before Piper has a chance to get heated.

We get through the routine on the first try, even Dreya. It's incredible that she was able to learn all those steps. I think she was embarrassed because her little groupies were down with it.

"Can we please get something to eat now?" DeShawn says. "I am hungry den a mug."

"So am I!" Meagan concurs.

"Are we doing room service or what?" I ask. "I'm too tired to go back out."

Sam says, "I'm with Sunday. Room service sounds great."

"Don't worry, y'all. We'll charge it to the room," I say when everyone looks at me kind of strange.

"Do you think you should run that by Mystique or Evan?" Dreya asks.

Since when did she care about spending money? Especially someone else's money! And I know she's not about to start acting like she's the good girl, on the straight and narrow, and that wild Sunday is the one spending up the money all recklessly.

"They expect for us to eat, Dreya. That's not a big deal."

"I just don't think Evan would want them eating room service. It's expensive, and he would rather spend the money on more important things than food and beverage."

Okay, now this is really feeling trippy, like some kind of alternate Twilight Zone reality.

"How do you know so much about what Evan wants?" Sam asks the obvious question that was hovering at the forefront of my mind.

"We had a long talk and he's about his business. Don't get mad at me because Evan and I connected. He's about to change the game and I'm trying to change it with him. That's real talk."

Kiki gives Dreya a fist pound. "That's what's up," Kiki says.

"Okay, for the sake of everyone's sanity, I'll call him and see what he says."

I take my cell phone and step out of the conference room. I don't want everyone to hear the conversation in case it goes in a direction I'm not trying to have it go, although I don't see what the big deal would be.

"Sunday, how's it going in Destin?" Evan asks without even saying hello.

"It's going well. Hey, I just wanted to run something by you before I do it, because I don't want there to be any issues."

"Okay, go ahead."

"We've been practicing all afternoon to get this choreography down, and the crew has done a fabulous job. I'm going to email you and Mystique a video of the rehearsal."

"Fantastic! And Drama was able to hook up with you too?"

"Yes. Surprisingly she was very cooperative."

"Surprisingly? You thought that she wouldn't want to work with you?"

"She hasn't in the past."

I can hear Evan sigh through the phone. "Why are you holding her to her past? If we're going to go forward like a family then we're going to have to let go of past hurts."

Okay, first of all Dreya is my *real* family. There's no record label that can make us any closer than we already are. We're blood.

"I'm not holding on to anything. I'm just happy she's moved on, so we can all do what we need to do."

"That's what I like to hear."

"So, I wanted to ask you, since the team has worked so hard, if you had an objection to us getting room service. They don't really feel like getting dressed to go back out."

"Room service, huh? Pizza Hut doesn't deliver to your hotel?"

"Um . . . well . . . I'm sure it does, but I want to reward everyone for their dedication."

"Aren't you paying them to be on the show?"

"Yes?"

"Aren't you allowing them the opportunity to be seen around the world?"

"Um . . . yes, I suppose."

"You suppose? You aren't sure?"

This conversation is going down a slippery slope into the tremendously irksome. "I am sure. Are you telling me you don't want me to do the room service? Let's cut to the chase."

I hear Evan chuckle. "Let me say this. If you decide to feed everyone room service, steak and lobster, like a big dog, trying to show off, then it will be your decision. But I will say that it's coming out of your royalty money."

"Why don't you check your books, Evan? I've made a lot of money and hardly spent any. I should have quite a bit at my disposal."

"You're right, Sunday. You have been thrifty, and I like that in you. You haven't done anything flashy, or blown a lot of money on stupid stuff. I just don't want you to start. It's addictive, and that's how the best of the best end up broke."

"You would know something about that, wouldn't you? Isn't that what happened to your last crew? They ended up broke?"

"Zac told me that you were the real deal, and that I wouldn't be able to just tell you anything and have you obey. So, since you've got a good head on your shoulders, I will treat you like I'm talking to my equal. Yes, they ended up broke. They were a bunch of drug-abusing idiots. Reign Records is going to be different."

"Okay, I believe you. But I'm making a decision tonight, to allow my crew to eat what they want. They deserve it. I deserve it."

"Just don't think of me as your enemy, Sunday," Evan says. "We're all on the same team."

"All right. I will talk to you later."

We're all on the same team? Hmmm . . . I don't know if I can believe that yet. This industry is beyond cutthroat, and everybody does what they have to do to survive. Something tells me that Evan isn't above playing dirty to come out on top.

14

Ms. Layla, Mystique's mother and fashion designer, has brought an entire collection of dresses to Zac's house for Mystique, Dreya, and I to try on for our red-carpet gowns. Evan says that we have to use Ms. Layla whether we want to or not, because Epsilon is picking up the tab for this. He's a serious penny pincher, which I don't mind, if the money is passed on to us. If he's just cutting corners to line his own pockets then I have a serious issue with his thriftiness.

"Drama and Sunday, I think you each need at least three looks," Ms. Layla says. "Of course your red-carpet look, your award-acceptance look, and your performance look. Each of these three will have different hair and makeup to accompany them."

"Mom, did you interview the makeup artists?"

"Yes, we found a perfect one. She did Toni Braxton's last tour. She's incredible."

"What about Regina?" I ask. "She's the only one who's ever done my makeup."

Ms. Layla and Mystique look at one another, but Mystique answers. "We had to fire Regina."

"What?" I ask. "Why?"

Mystique clears her throat and strides across the room to look at some of the dresses. "Some things came to my attention about Regina. She was spreading some untruths about me and Zac. I can't have someone like that in my circle. She had to go."

Dreya laughs out loud. "Dang, Mystique be putting chicks out! Fired her? What did she say about you that was *that* bad? I mean, y'all corny as what anyway."

"That's not important," Mystique says. "What's important is that she betrayed my trust. I let her into my inner circle and she abused that right."

"What is this? The mob?" Dreya asks. "You gangsta like a big dawg!"

"I protect mine, and I handle business when necessary," Mystique says. "Nothing gangsta about that."

I don't say anything about the firing. I'm wondering if anyone told Mystique about what Regina said to me. There was no one there but us, and I know that I didn't say anything. Maybe it wasn't the only thing Regina was talking greasy about.

"Well, can someone communicate to the new makeup artist that I do not and will not do fake eyelashes?" I say.

"You ain't gonna take up for your girl, Regina?" Dreya asks. "That's your homegirl, right?"

I shrug. "I'm sure that Mystique had a good reason to fire her. I'm not going to question that right now."

"So, Sunday," Ms. Layla says. "I love your skin tone in warm colors. Fall is your season. How about this copper tube dress for the red carpet?"

I look at the tiny piece of material that Ms. Layla holds up. "That's a dress? Where is the rest of it?" I ask.

"It stretches, honey. Try it on."

I snatch off my jeans and T-shirt and pull the little sliver of material over my underwear. It's a good thing that I'm naturally thin, because this dress doesn't hide a dang thing. It clings to my stomach like a piece of Saran wrap on a hunk of meat.

"That's hot," Dreya says.

I disagree. "Ms. Layla. I'm not feeling this. I need something with a little more . . . coverage."

Ms. Layla chuckles. "When I was your age, I was the same way. Always covering up. Now I wish I had that body!"

Dreya says, "I want a tiny dress just like that, but not that color. I only want to cover up the vital parts."

"I've got the perfect outfit for you, Drama."

Ms. Layla pulls a red and black skintight halter dress from the rack. Dreya claps her hands and squeals.

"That's what I'm talking about!" Dreya says. "That's what's up!"

"We're gonna get you some black fishnet stockings and leather booties. Your long legs are going to look divine."

"What about my hair? How will I wear my hair with this?"

Mystique says, "I'm thinking a big, red updo, with curls cascading down in the back."

"That's hot," Dreya says. "And of course, I've got to have my red lipstick."

"Certainly," Ms. Layla says. "You can't go without that."

I rifle through the dresses until I find one that I like. It's a cream-colored knee-length satin number. It is perfect for me.

"I like this one," I say. "I look good in cream."

Ms. Layla takes the dress from my hands. "Well, honey, Mystique is wearing cream on the red carpet. I want the two of you to be colorful, in case someone tries to photograph all three of you at once."

Mystique is wearing cream? Why is it that all of a sudden I'm feeling like a second fiddle to Mystique? I never got that vibe until recently. Maybe it's been going on the entire time, and I've just been too giddy about having a record deal to even notice.

"Okay, well, let me keep looking, because that copper thing ain't getting it," I say.

Finally, I come to another gown that I like. It is a deep orange kimono, with gold and brown writing on it. It's floor length, and completely elegant. Not something I'd wear normally, but definitely something I can rock.

"What about this one?" I ask. "Will it take anything away from Mystique's outfit?"

"What does that mean?" Mystique asks.

"Nothing. I just want to be sure we don't clash. You know. For the pictures."

Mystique narrows her eyes at me as if trying to read my mind and figure out if I'm innocent, or if there's a deeper meaning to my words. She can squint all day, but I'm going to keep giving her this wide-eyed gaze and silly grin. She'll never be able to figure me out.

"That won't clash at all," Ms. Layla says. "Actually, it's quite lovely. I'm sure that would be wonderful on you, after a few alterations. I think it was cut to fit Mystique and she's a little bit wider than you in the hip and stomach areas."

"I am not!" Mystique objects.

It takes everything in me not to burst into laughter, but Dreya doesn't even try to contain herself. She doubles over at the waist and lets the laughs ripple out of her body.

"Your mother called you fat!" Dreya roars.

"No, she didn't!" Mystique yells.

"Don't get mad at me, fatty. You shouldn't have been eating all that steak and lobster with Zac. A moment on the lips, an eternity on the hips!"

"Okay, Drama. That is enough. Mystique, honey, you have one of the best bodies in this industry," Ms. Layla says. "Women are going into plastic surgeons' offices carrying your picture, saying I want to look like this."

"Was the picture Photoshopped?" Dreya asks with laughter still pouring out of her.

Mystique jumps up and gets right in Dreya's face. Dreya's laughter stops. Immediately.

"You think that just because you're hooking up with Evan that you can talk to me any kind of way? I will have you dropped from this label so fast your weaved-up little head will spin!"

Screech! What? OMG! I should've known something was going on when Dreya showed up on our Destin trip acting like she was in the know with Evan. Because she really, really was in the know! Shut the front door!

Dreya smiles at Mystique. "I want to see you try, heffa.

Evan is on to you. He doesn't like how you try to hold back every new artist. He sees what you're doing. Just like you don't have Bethany here to get a dress for the red carpet. I already texted Evan about that."

"She doesn't need a red-carpet dress! She's not even nominated for anything."

Dreya shakes her head. "Evan wants everyone from Reign Records to come up in the spot looking like royalty. That's our calling card."

"Who do you think you are?" Mystique roars with anger. She sounds like a lioness about to strike that weak little antelope that all the rest of the herd left behind.

"I am Ms. Drama, soon to be the queen of Reign Records. You know what? I don't want to wear any of these tacky creations. What about you, Sunday? Do you want a real designer to create your look? One that's not related to Mystique the hater?"

I don't know why Dreya's trying to rope me into this. I want no part of beef with anyone. Not Mystique and definitely not Evan, since my career, at this point, is in the palm of his hand.

"You know that I don't really give a care about what I wear to an awards show. It makes absolutely no difference."

Dreya stands and drops Ms. Layla's dress on the floor like a piece of garbage. "I'll see myself out," she says.

After she slams the door, Mystique says, "She is going to ruin everything we've worked for. Everything."

"I had no idea she was with him. I feel like I'm totally in the dark. No wonder she got put in my performance at the last minute," I say. "I really wish you'd said something to me, Mystique."

"I should've. I'm sorry. I was hoping that he'd dump her and that would be the end of it. Evan uses women like he uses toilet paper, so I thought she'd just be a one and done."

"Evan is only one third of the Epsilon Records decision-making partners," Ms. Layla says. "You all just have to make sure that you have Caterina and Lawrence on your side."

"Caterina will be the hardest to sway," Mystique says. "She only speaks dollars and cents. If Drama's antics make them money, then she'll be all for whatever she does."

I roll my eyes. "Well, what about Lawrence?"

"He's dedicated to art. He's the reason we've been able to sign artists like you and Bethany. He hears raw talent like yours and goes bananas. He's about the musical legacy."

"Then he's our guy. He's the one we want to be in good with."

Mystique smiles. "I'm already in good with Lawrence. Don't worry. He's the company owner's son, too, so there won't be any getting rid of him by Evan. Evan knows he has to play nice with Lawrence."

"This is too much! I just want to make music. I don't want to have strategies or plans that include making alliances."

"Unfortunately, that's how it goes, Sunday. You're going to have to get used to it," Ms. Layla says.

"I want people to be honest with me. I can take the truth, even if it's crazy. Just give it to me straight."

Mystique nods. "I will always do that."

"Then tell me why you fired Regina, and not that cryptic mess you said before. The real reason."

Mystique moves from the ornate antique chaise, to sit next to me on the couch. "It's like this. Regina talks too much, and not everything she says is true."

"Specifics, Mystique. You're still talking in riddles."

"Okay, she told another one of the stylists that Zac set Sam up with that chick at the club that put something in his drink. He had nothing to do with it."

"Wow!" I reply with fake surprise. "Why would anyone accuse Zac of something like that? I don't even think I'd believe it if I heard it."

"Well, that's why we fired her. Big D wasn't happy about it, because he was messing with her."

"Whatever! Get out of here! He's about to marry Shelly."

I also suspected this about Big D, but I wasn't going to tell Mystique that I'm that perceptive. While she thinks she's filling me in on the scoop, I let her. I just want to see how much she'll spill and if I'll get anything else that I don't already know.

"Now, more than ever before, we've got to make sure our circle is tight. We can't let anyone come between us, Sunday. I have to know that you've got my back, and please know that I've got yours."

"Sometimes . . . I . . . never mind." I start to tell Mystique how I feel she does things to play me out, but then I think better of it.

"You can say anything to me," Mystique says.

"Well, I just wanted to say that sometimes I can't believe all this is real. I'm still trying to wrap my head around having three number-one hits and an American Music Award nomination. All this extra stuff with my cousin is like so unnecessary."

"Exactly. You wait until you get your royalty check, Sunday. You are a very wealthy young lady. You'll be able to buy anything you want. You can actually buy whatever you want now. Epsilon will give you credit."

I shake my head. "No, I don't want to work like that. I want to spend my money when it's in my hand. That way I can keep better track of it."

Mystique's smile is large and bright. So bright that it looks almost fake. "See, Sunday, you don't have to worry about Evan. He may have destroyed his other artists, but he's never seen the likes of us. There's no way he's going to pimp us and leave us dry."

"That's an interesting term . . . pimp."

"Yes, that's what he does. Evan lets these artists spend more money than they have so that they're always in debt to the record company. Once they start living a certain lifestyle, they can't stop. It's like they're addicted to it, but his artists never earned the money to have that life."

"That will never be me!"

"I hope not, sweetie, because that's a sad situation," Ms. Layla says. "I've seen it too many times."

Making it big and losing it all is definitely not how I roll. I didn't come this far to end up broke. My mama taught me well. I don't need a Mystique, a Ms. Layla, or an Evan to keep me on the right path.

It's kind of amazing that Dreya and I grew up together, but turned out so differently.

15

——————

"Mom, do you want to go to the American Music Awards with us?" I ask my mother as I lay stretched out on her living room couch. This was always one of my favorite places to lounge, because there is a direct line of sight from the couch to the TV.

My mother wipes her flour covered hands on her apron. She's making my favorite, fried chicken and waffles.

"No, I don't think so. That's next weekend right?"

I nod. "I didn't think you'd want to go, but Dreya is bringing Aunt Charlie, so I just wanted to make sure you weren't mad at me."

"Going to an awards show with a bunch of artists would not be my thing, but your aunt . . . well, I'm sure she'll enjoy herself."

"And embarrass everybody too! Aunt Charlie gets on my nerves."

"Oh, I think she's planning to be really classy this time. She and Dreya went shopping for some platinum-blond weave."

I shake my head and change the channel on the TV. My mom is just saying this to get on my nerves. She knows that I hate Aunt Charlie's colorful weaves.

"I wish that just once, Aunt Charlie would buy hair in a color that grows naturally from humans' heads."

This makes my mother laugh. "Charlie is just trying to stay young. Y'all growing up is making us feel old."

"Excuse me!" My baby cousin, Manny, is tapping on my foot with an action figure of some sort. I look up at him and he's got a really stank expression on his face.

"I want to go to the America Awards!" Manny says.

"You can't go, lil' man! This is just for grown people."

"Then why you going? You ain't grown. I just heard my mama telling Dreya the other day that her name *ain't* Drama and she ain't grown. Since my sister is older than you that means you ain't grown either!"

My mom says, "Sunday goes to college. Doesn't that make her all grown up?"

"Nope, 'cause she still be over here eating our food. And she don't have a job!"

I hit Manny with a little pillow from the couch and he jabs the action figure into my leg. "You little monster! I do have a job. I am a singer, remember?"

"Oh, yeah. You and Dreya be going on tour and stuff. But when you gone get a check? People who be on TV is not supposed to be living with roaches."

"Manny, we do not have roaches," my mother says.

"For real? I thought I saw one in my oatmeal this morning. That's why I ain't eat it."

"Boy, that was a raisin!" my mother says as she chases Manny out of the room.

As much as I'm enjoying college life and the dorm, I miss Manny's little self. Always eating my food, falling asleep in my bed, and then peeing on himself and wetting up my sheets. Wait a minute. What the heck am I saying? I do not miss this at all!

"Are you going to be back home for Thanksgiving? All of this traveling to California and whatnot is taking place right around the holidays."

"It is. But the awards show is on November twenty-first. We'll be back home in plenty of time to eat your turkey, dressing, and macaroni and cheese."

"Who's we? Is Sam going to come to our Thanksgiving feast?"

"He probably will."

"How's my Sam?" my mother asks. "How's he doing in school?"

"He dropped out, Mom! Can you believe that?"

"I'm sure he had a good reason. The last time I spoke to his mother she said he was making almost a six-figure salary."

"You talk to Sam's mother?" This is somewhat annoying. I don't know if I want my mother all up in my mix, calling my boyfriend's mother like she's checking up on me. Parents are nosy as what!

"I saw her at the steppers ball."

"What in the world is a steppers ball? Sounds like some old people party."

"It's a party where we play our music and do our dances. Stepping."

"So why were you two talking about me and Sam?"

My mother laughs out loud. "We can talk about you if we want! He's paying some of his mother's bills and she's happy about that. But she doesn't like him living all the way in New York City."

"Me either."

"It must be nice for her, though, getting some of those bills paid."

I have to cover my mouth with my hand to keep from laughing out loud. My mother is hinting at getting her bills paid, which is absolutely a given when I finally get a royalty check.

"Mom, when I get my money, you know I'm gonna hook you up!"

"Dreya got an advance check. You didn't get one of those and didn't tell me, did you?"

"No, Mom! I took a small advance to pay for my tuition. I don't want to borrow against my earnings. I want to be shocked when I hold that check in my hand. Mystique says it's going to be pretty large."

"We'll get an accountant and plan it out before you spend one dime. I don't want you to look up and still not have enough money for school. Not after all of this."

"Me either, because finishing school is like my prime directive right now. That's why I don't understand what's up with Sam."

"Maybe you'll find that it's hard to keep up with both as well. I mean, you're going to an award show in the middle of your semester. How can you concentrate on your studies with all of this going on?"

"It's hard. But I don't want to quit."

"Just know that whatever you do, I'll support you one hundred percent. But I don't want to see you burn out."

"I will stop doing music before I drop out of school."

My mother moves my legs out of the way and sits down next to me. "You know, every decision is not black and white. Some things are kind of hazy."

"What are you saying?"

"I'm just saying that I don't want you to be so dead set on one decision that you miss a blessing from God."

"You think God wants me to drop out of college?"

My mother shrugs. "I'm not sure, but He'll give you a sign about it, that I do know."

I lay back on the couch and gaze at the ceiling, trying to digest my mother's words of wisdom. I would think that if *anyone* wanted me to stay at Spelman, it would be my mom. Everyone's doubting me before they give me a chance to succeed.

I'm going to show them. My mother, Sam, Mystique, Evan . . . all of them. I can and will do this: school and the music. I will be the exception to the rule. I'm going to be the one to prove everyone wrong.

16

"I'm Jessica Barnes from Younggiftedandrich.com and I'm coming to you live and direct from the red carpet of the American Music Awards, at the Nokia Theatre in beautiful Los Angeles. They say that it never rains in Southern California, but we're getting a few raindrops this evening. But a little bit of rain is not keeping the stars from shining bright. I've got Sunday Tolliver, rising star and princess of Reign Records. Tell us who designed your fabulous geisha-inspired gown."

I inhale deeply and exhale. I realize this is going to be on the Internet in front of thousands of people and I feel my nerves getting the best of me.

"Thank you! It was designed by none other than Ms. Layla."

"Now, Ms. Layla is Mystique's mother, right?"

"Yes, and she designs wonderful clothes."

"Did she outfit everyone here from Reign Records tonight?"

"Not everyone, but quite a few."

Actually, she designed clothes for everyone except Dreya, but I'm not going to say that to the interviewer for this very, very popular blog. They get close to a million hits a day and the last thing I want is to be quoted starting drama.

"Sooo . . . this is Sam, your boyfriend, right?"

A big smile on my face as Sam puts his arm around me. He says, "I'm the executive producer on her album. We wrote every song together."

Jessica giggles. "Well, you make very beautiful music together."

"Thank you," I say, before we're pushed forward on the red carpet, and Jessica attacks some other more popular celebrities.

I whisper to Sam, "Did you see? That was Patti La-Belle. I want to meet her later."

"I want to meet Lauryn Hill. Maybe she'll ask me to work on her next project. That would be hot!"

"Ooh! Look! There's Alicia Keys and Beyoncé! I wonder what they're talking about."

"Beyoncé? Hmm . . . she just reminds me so much of Mystique. I don't know."

Sam and I make our way to the doors of the building, stopping periodically to take pictures. Sam is cracking me up! He makes sure he's got his arm around my waist on every picture. He just wants everyone to know that we're together.

When we get inside the auditorium Sam and I are led to seats close to the stage. There are little tags on each seat, and I notice that every seat in our row is a Reign Records or Epsilon Records artist. I'm sitting between Dreya and Sam.

A distraught-looking usher leads Dreya and Dilly to their seats. Dreya looks beautiful in her red and black (I guess she liked the colors, just not Ms. Layla's dress), but I think I can almost see the steam rising from her head.

"Do you know they would not let my mother onto the red carpet?" Dreya fusses.

I chuckle at the thought of Aunt Charlie posing on the red carpet and talking to bloggers. I know Dreya doesn't like it, but it was really for the best that Aunt Charlie was not allowed her moment to shine.

"It's okay, Dreya. Auntie is not a celebrity."

"But they not gonna disrespect my mother, Sunday. You would've been tripping if that was Auntie Shawn."

Actually, my mother wouldn't want to come anywhere near a red carpet. She didn't even want her face shown on our reality show. My mom is kind of low-key, so I guess that's where I get it from. Dreya . . . well, she's definitely a lot like her mother!

Dreya starts to say something else, but then she clutches my arm. "What is *he* doing here? I didn't think he'd show up!"

The "he" that Dreya is referring to is her ex-boyfriend, and American Music Award–nominated rapper, Truth. I don't know why she didn't think he'd show up, just because he got dropped from Epsilon Records. He still does music, so it makes perfect sense for him to be here.

His long locks are tied neatly in the back and he's wearing a suit. I don't think I've ever seen him dressed up. He's got not one, but two video chicks escorting him, like he's some sort of don. He actually looks quite ridiculous.

"I told Evan that we should've come together," Dreya hisses as Truth's girls pose for pictures with him right in the auditorium.

"You don't have to prove anything to him. Don't worry about it," I say.

I feel Sam jab me in my back. I know he wants an explanation about Dreya and Evan, but I can't give it to him right now, so I just jab him back.

Dilly says, "You want me to pretend to be your date. I won't try to feel you up or anything."

"Ewww! Get away from me, boy. You wish I'd let you pretend to be my date."

More and more celebrities come into the auditorium and I'm in awe of how glamorous everyone looks. Big D comes in with Shelly, and her dress reminds me of colored Saran wrap. She's working it though, with her bling and her fabulous shoes.

Big D and Shelly are sitting in the row behind us, and Shelly kisses me on the cheek when they locate their seats. "Ain't seen you in a few days, Sunday. Come over next week and I'll make you some fried chicken and macaroni and cheese."

"That's what's up!"

Sam taps his chest. "What about me? I still like chicken! I still like mac and cheese."

Shelly laughs and gives Sam a friendly kiss on his forehead like an old lady would give a little boy. "Are you going to even be in Atlanta next week?"

"Yes, I am. So you can just save me some of that food, Shelly. I'm not playing."

A loud amount of chatter in the room starts when Mystique, Zac, Evan, and some random girl walk into the auditorium. Evan is clearly coupled up with the girl. She's definitely not an artist, but not your regular garden-variety groupie either. She looks like a model type, and Dreya is not happy.

She's furious.

"I cannot believe him!" she fusses under her breath.

One thing about Dreya is that she does not know how to hide her feelings. At all. So while she doesn't say anything to Evan, the icy glare she gives him lets him know that something is going on.

Surprisingly she doesn't explode. This is typically the kind of venue where Dreya likes to show her behind.

"Are you okay?" I whisper to her as we sit down for the show's opening.

"I'm fine. I'm not going to let a groupie ruin my career."

For the first hour of the show we watch singers, rappers, and actors take the stage distributing and receiving awards. Mystique wins for Best R & B Artist.

Dreya stands up to join Mystique, and Mystique gives her an evil expression, like she wants to punch her in the face. So, I guess it's safe to say that Mystique is ignoring her own decree about all of the Reign Records artists coming on stage for all of the awards.

I listen to her speech. She thanks just about everyone

in our camp, from Evan down to Big D and of course
Zac.

"... and I want to give a very special thank you to some
very gifted songwriters, Sunday Tolliver, Sam Wilkins,
Jayquon X, and Selena Bryant. I wouldn't have had such
great hit songs without your tremendous talent."

I glance down the row at Evan and his mouth forms a
grim line across his face. He's clearly not happy, and I
know it has to do with the fact that Mystique didn't invite all of us up on stage with her. Not even the groupie
fawning all over Evan seems to be making him feel better.

After the first hour of the show, we go backstage to
prepare for our performance. It's the first time I've seen
my friends all night. Gia and Piper have huge grins on
their faces and everybody looks excited.

Gia runs up and gives me a hug. "Girl, you were fly as
what on the red carpet! We watched you from back here.
Also, do you know how many celebrities we met back
here! My autograph book is full and Piper got a date."

"With who?"

"Some rapper in Truth's entourage. They invited her to
an after-party. . . ."

I walk away from Gia midsentence, stride over to
Piper, and grab her by the arm. "Piper. Truth's crew is
bad news. Seriously. You can go with us, after the show.
We're going to an after-party too."

"Sunday, I'm cool. I can take care of myself. I might
not even go with them! I didn't say yes, I just took the
guy's cell phone number. Don't stress about it."

Piper snatches her arm away from me and gives me a
look of sheer irritation. Maybe I overstepped the bound-

aries of our friendship. I mean, I've only known her for a couple of months and now I'm trying to tell her who she should or shouldn't kick it with.

"My bad, Piper. I was just worried about you. That's all."

"I got this. I've been taking care of me since I was five years old."

Piper walks away, and I don't follow her even though I feel like I should say something else. I don't know what that would be, though. I guess I'm so used to being the one person in my circle with any common sense. Dealing with Dreya and Bethany left me feeling that way.

Speaking of Bethany, even though she's not in my routine, she's backstage and talking to Evan. She's dressed similarly to the other dancers in my group, so I'm wondering if she's coming out on stage with us. I wouldn't care, but I know she didn't learn the routine. Dilly is on the opposite side of the dressing room, giving Bethany cautious glances.

I walk up to them and hug Bethany. "Hey, girl. What's going on?"

"Well . . ."

Evan interjects, "Do you mind if she joins you on-stage? She can lead the backup singers."

"I know the song, Sunday," Bethany adds.

"Sure, but I don't see the point. She's a solo artist. Why would she want to come out and sing backup with me on stage?"

Evan says, "It's the message we're sending about Reign Records. When they see all of you on stage together—you, Drama, Dilly, and Bethany—it will show that all past bad blood has been erased. Especially since Truth is no longer in the picture."

I shrug. It actually sounds like a good idea, and since I don't really trust Evan, that's saying a lot for me.

Evan continues, "Mystique has shown that she's not down for the family, but we've got to make sure we still have a good showing for Reign Records tonight."

Uh-oh. I knew that Evan was annoyed with Mystique about the whole coming on stage thing, but I didn't know he was *this* mad about it. Evan standing backstage dissing Mystique to a couple of newbies is not a good look.

A gossip blogger who's scammed her way backstage takes pictures of Evan as he talks to the other artists and dancers and she's recording him with her camera phone. He doesn't seem to care, but I do. I've got my eye on her. I don't want her anywhere near me.

I ask Bethany, "Did you and Dilly work everything out?"

"Girl, yeah. He thinks I'm gone over him."

"Are you?"

"What? Be serious, Sunday. I thought you knew me better than that. I liked him and everything, and of course I wanted to know why he wanted to break up, but I'm straight."

"So you're okay working with him?"

"Look at him! You should be asking him that question. He's been standing in the corner, terrified like a little punk since I got back here. He acts like I'm gonna do something to him. I'm trying to get this paper."

I chuckle under my breath, because Bethany sounds just like me, talking about getting this paper. To look at her, you'd think she was straight Disney Channel with all that straight brown hair and blond highlights. Her makeup is all glittery and pink. She looks like an extra on the *Hannah Montana* show or something. But as soon as she opens her mouth it's straight hood.

"Okay, well, maybe you should tell him it's all good."

Bethany laughs. "Nope. I'm actually enjoying this. That's what he gets for trying to play me with his young self. I should've known to not kick it with a high school senior."

"Yeah, college boys are better," I say.

"Or I could do like Dreya and get myself a grown man that's making paper. Forget boys altogether."

I don't comment on this since Evan is at the awards show with a groupie. I don't know what's going through Dreya's mind on that topic, but I know it can't be good. She's never been one to share.

"You guys are on in ten minutes," the production assistant says.

"Is everyone ready?" I ask.

"Everyone except you, Sunday," Ms. Layla says. "You need to get into your stage costume."

Ms. Layla has me dressed and made up in about four minutes flat. She's great at that whole quick-change operation thing.

Next thing I know, we're on stage in front of all these people. This is worse than a concert of fans. This is the entire music industry waiting to see if we can bring it.

And guess what?

We totally bring it!

After the first chorus, we have planned Dreya's rap break, but when Dilly steps to the microphone too, I'm surprised.

He and Dreya go back and forth on the mic, wowing the crowd with their incredible lyrics. I didn't write one line in the entire rap. Maybe Dreya does have the talent to write her own hits.

Everyone stands to their feet when I start the second verse, and Bethany's background vocals ring out loud when she harmonizes with me on a few notes like we used to do back in the day.

When we get a standing ovation by the crowd, I am shocked and humbled. It's like they accept us into the music scene! We're the newbies, and we're being welcomed with open arms.

Finally, it's time to present the T-Mobile Breakthrough Artist of the Year award. I didn't know how much I wanted to win until they started reading off the nominees' names.

I hold my breath as the presenter says, "And the winner is . . . Sunday Tolliver."

I sit frozen in place when she says my name! Did she really just say me? Did I really just win an American Music Award when I just started in the music business not even a year ago?

When I don't jump out of my seat, everyone in my row hauls me up! Unlike Mystique, I want, and *need*, everybody to come up on stage with me. Sam hugs me tight and holds my hand as we go up to the stage.

I know that everyone is expecting a speech, but I stand in front of the microphone for a moment, trying to think of what to say.

"Wow . . . I didn't write anything, because I didn't think I would win. So, I'm just gonna wing it up here. I want to thank God, because . . . y'all just don't know what I went through last year. I was at a place . . . um . . . I didn't think I would be able to go to college, and then everything happened so fast. Big D, Mystique, Zillionaire, Evan, Caterina, Lawrence, and everyone at Reign Records, thank you so much for this opportunity! Thank you, BET, for producing the reality shows that put us on the map. To all of the fans who bought the album as soon as it was released on iTunes and Amazon and everywhere else—I appreciate you for not bootlegging! To my crew who hold it all the way down, my cousin Drama, Bethany, Dilly, Gia, Piper, Meagan, DeShawn, and Ricky, y'all are the best! Hey Aunt Charlie and Manny! To my mommy, I love you! And last but definitely not least, Sam, you are the best songwriting partner I could ever want or dream of having. We did this together, so I share this award with you. And . . . I hope we keep making beautiful music together."

The applause is thunderous! I hope no one from the audience can see the tears streaming down my face.

Everything right now is so . . . perfect! I wish that I could just stay in this moment for the rest of my life.

17

This after-party is jumping. Epsilon has rented out an entire nightclub for all of their artists and every label on their line. New artists are performing and it's wall-to-wall beautiful people here. And my aunt Charlie is in the middle of it all.

I tried to get Dreya to talk her into going back to the hotel, to enjoy room service and the cable TV. But Aunt Charlie wasn't having it. She came to Los Angeles to get her party on. Even if the majority of people in this room are at least twenty years younger than she is.

The good thing about Aunt Charlie is that she's fly as ever. I've got to give it to her, the platinum wig is on point with its loose spiral curls that wave down her back. Her dress is cold too! It's black and skin tight. My auntie has a banging body and while she doesn't look as young as we do, she definitely doesn't look her age.

Aunt Charlie is already on the dance floor when I get there with my crew. She's got a very young-looking guy grinding all up on her, and she's enjoying every second of it.

"Look at your mom!" Bethany says to Dreya as we walk in. "She is getting it in!"

Dreya shakes her head. "That's how she rolls. She never got to have a lot of fun when she was our age, because she had me. So just let her kick it!"

I guess. I'm just glad it's not my mother out there. If Dreya is okay with it, then I guess I am too.

Sam is still holding my hand. He hasn't let me go since I won the award. I was surprised that Dreya congratulated me. I was afraid that she was going to be angry that she didn't win. But she seemed cool with it, so maybe everything is back to normal between me and my cousin.

Dreya's friends Kiki and Tasia walk into the party with wide eyes like two little kids at Willy Wonka's Chocolate Factory or something. Tasia came ready to catch a baller with her sheer lace dress. Underneath the black lace she's wearing a pair of shiny boy shorts and a tiny, tiny bra. Very little is left to the imagination.

Even Kiki, who seems most comfortable in jeans, a button-down shirt, and a tank top, dressed up. She's got on a tiny skirt and cute ruffled blouse. She does look uncomfortable as what wearing those high-heel shoes, and as soon as we're on the dance floor for two minutes she takes the shoes off and holds them in her hand.

"How do y'all dance in these things?" she asks me as she slips the heels on her hands.

"I don't dance in them. I dance in flats!"

Sam pulls me away from the crowd, and I realize that we're following Evan into the VIP area. When we get into the sealed off room, Mystique, Zac, and Big D are there, as well as the executives from Epsilon Records. Finally, Evan is claiming Dreya for the evening. He escorts her to his private table, where the champagne is flowing freely.

Sam whispers to me, "You know that's trouble, right?"

I nod, but don't reply. I really wish that my cousin would make the right choices for who she wants to date. No one can tell her anything, but in this case, I'm sure Aunt Charlie would be all for it!

Dreya waves her hand at Sam and I. "Come over here with me!" she says.

Evan nods at Sam to let him know it's okay and we go over to Evan's table to sit down. I notice that Mystique follows us with her eyes, and she's expressionless. I wonder what she's thinking, because I know she's not feeling Evan right now.

"Sunday, guess what?" Dreya says with an excited expression on her face.

"What?"

"I'm moving to New York with Evan."

My mouth drops open as I sit down. "Get the heck outta here! Are you serious? Then . . . why was he at the award show with that other chick?"

"She was a hired escort. He can't go public with us like that. Not yet. But we will in time."

I can't imagine my cousin moving to New York City.

"Now, I'll be able to keep an eye on Sam for you, and make sure he's not getting with any random chicks."

Sam rolls his eyes. "Whatever, Dreya. I don't need anyone watching me. You can go 'head with that."

Dreya laughs out loud. "Dang, Sam! I'm just playing. I'm not gonna have time to worry about what you and Zac are doing anyway. I'm going to be too busy living it up!"

"What did Aunt Charlie say?"

"At first she wasn't feeling it, but when Evan gave her the deed and keys to a new house in Lithonia, she changed her mind."

"OMG! He bought your mother a house?"

"Yep. It's a little three-bedroom bungalow, but it's big enough for her and Manny and even Auntie Shawn if she wants to come with them. It has a pool too!"

I know that my mother will be happy beyond belief that her sister will have a home of her own. I also know that she would never want to live with her.

Something about Evan and his generosity just seems strange to me. It feels like he's trying to buy Aunt Charlie's support, but that is totally unnecessary. Dreya does whatever she wants to do anyway. No one could've told her not to be with Evan or move to New York with him.

"I'm happy for Aunt Charlie. She hasn't had her own place in a while. Did y'all get Manny Transformers stuff for his room? You know that's what he likes."

Dreya laughs out loud. "Yes, that little runt's room is tricked all the way out in Transformers stuff. I even got him a new comforter, so he can throw that other one away. It's probably saturated with pee anyway."

Now this makes me laugh! One day poor Manny is

gonna get us back for all this teasing about his bed wetting.

"Y'all want some champagne?" Dreya asks as she
pours herself another glass.

"No, and don't you think you've had enough? Last
time I checked we were still under age," I say.

"Boo!" Dreya says. "Stop being a party killer. Nobody
is about to get drunk on champagne, Sunday."

"Maybe not, but still no thanks."

"Suit yourself."

Evan stands in the middle of the room with a cham-
pagne-filled glass raised to the sky. "Hey, everybody. Let's
lift our glasses up to celebrate the wins from Epsilon
Records artists tonight. Mystique with three wins, the
Bama Boys with their phenomenal sweep in the country
categories, and our new princess of Reign Records, Sunday Tolliver!"

Everyone hurries to get glasses in hand to raise the
toast with Evan. Mystique's frown deepens after she
takes a sip of champagne and sets her glass down. This
thing between her and Evan has the potential to turn into
a hot, steamy pile of drama. I hope it doesn't. I'm on a
drama break.

Mystique walks over to our table with her glass in
hand. She stops in front of me and kisses both my cheeks.
She ignores Dreya, which is completely okay, I think, because Dreya ignores her too. There's a mutual dislike
going on there.

"Congratulations, Sunday. You deserved that Breakthrough Artist award. No one has hustled harder this

year than you. None of the other nominees even came close to your shine."

Dreya grins because she gets the extreme diss from Mystique. Surprisingly, she doesn't respond to it.

"Thank you, Mystique! I think everybody in that category worked hard, even Truth. I wouldn't have been mad if someone else won. We're all grinding."

"That's for real," Sam says. "We're taking this hustle to new heights."

"Well, say what you want," Mystique says, "it takes more than hustle, or hooking up with someone famous to stay relevant in the game. You need talent too, and Sunday, you've got that part on lock. Don't let anybody tell you differently."

Mystique makes eye contact with another artist who waves her over. It's one of the Bama Boys. They want Mystique to do a duet with them on their Christmas album. I think that's going to be funny. An R & B star with a country-western group. But I see she's trying to maximize all streams of revenue and all fan bases. Can't be mad at that.

"I'll talk to you some more later, Sunday," Mystique says as she walks away.

As soon as she's out of listening range, Dreya bursts into laughter. "That heffa is so jealous of me and Evan. Do you know she wanted him before she got with Zac? She hooked up with him when she was on our level, trying to get in the game. How she gonna be hating on my come-up?"

I do not reply, because I don't want to get in this. Besides, I don't have an opinion on anything Mystique did or allegedly did before I knew her. It doesn't have anything to do with me, or Dreya for that matter. I also am not going to give Dreya my thoughts on her hook up with Evan. I think it's a mistake. Clearly she thinks it's the best decision she ever made.

"I guess we'll all see what worked or what didn't work ten years from now," Sam says. "Hopefully, we're all still living the fab life."

I nod in agreement. Whether it's singing on a stage or running a successful entertainment law practice, I'm going to be living the fabulous life. Because fab for me isn't fly parties, jewelry, big houses, or vacations. My fabulous is living life with the people I love, and not having to worry about how the bills get paid.

Actually, I think that is beyond fab!

18

Back on campus, Gia and Piper are getting a taste of the celebrity life when people come up and congratulate them for their performance on the American Music Awards.

We're sitting in the campus courtyard, trying to get some study in and being totally unsuccessful. First of all, the weather has finally turned, and there is a nip in the air—enough for us to wear sweaters and sweats. And Meagan just can't seem to concentrate without hating.

"It's not like you guys actually did anything, for crying out loud," Meagan says as she pulls her sweater tight around her body. "You were back-up dancers."

"Well, I was just happy to get a check!" Piper says. "Thanks, Sunday. Anytime you want me to work for you, just let me know. I can sing a little bit too."

"Really?" I ask. "Let me hear what you got."

Piper sings the first few lines of the "Star-Spangled Banner." Actually, she murders the first lines of the song. I have never heard such screeching in my life.

"You're kidding, right?" I ask.

Piper laughs out loud. "Wow. You are straight hating on my skills."

"I witnessed no skills," Gia says.

"Me either," Meagan says.

"Oh, guess what? The Gamma Phi Gamma girls are straight jocking me!" Gia says. "They want me to choreograph their routine for the spring step show."

Meagan replies, "That doesn't mean they're jocking you! They just know that you put together a slamming routine. It doesn't mean that they want you in the sorority either."

Gia laughs. "I don't care one way or the other. I was just sharing the news."

Piper asks, "Are we studying or aren't we? I've got to make sure I get good grades on these midterm exams. I've got a few scholarship applications pending, and I need to make sure my grades don't slip."

"Scholarships?" Meagan asks. "But you're already in school. You're still looking for scholarship money?"

"Yes, of course I am. I would like to stay in school and finish," Piper says. "Plus, my financial aid stuff is totally up in the air. I still can't find my mother."

"You should report her as a missing person," Gia says. "Will that help? How long have you not been able to reach her?"

"Since my senior year in high school. But my grandmother said she came through about a month ago and robbed her of her Social Security check, so it's not like she's hiding away in rehab or anything like that."

Meagan is always highly uncomfortable when we talk about Piper's family situation. She says, "I can't imagine growing up with a meth addict for a mother."

"Well, she wasn't always a meth addict," Piper explains. "She started off just drinking and smoking weed. Then she graduated to heroin, and when that got too expensive she downsized to crack and meth. Honestly, I'm surprised she's still alive."

"You don't sound sad about it," Meagan says.

"I am numb to it," Piper says. "She's not ever been around, so I know that she gave birth to me, but she doesn't feel like my mother."

My heart goes out to Piper. She tries to act so strong about her mother being on drugs, but I know that it hurts her. She's lucky to have her foster parents.

Piper says, "Listen, change the subject, okay? Talking about Stella is a real downer. Plus, I might be dating someone new, so that's a more fun thing to talk about, right?"

"Who is the someone new that you might be dating?" Gia asks.

"Remember the guy from Truth's entourage that asked me out on a date the night of the awards show?" Piper asks. "Well, he's in Atlanta and he goes to Georgia State."

"Get the heck out of here!" I say. "Truth has friends that go to college?"

"Turns out he's not really Truth's friend. He's Truth's

cousin. He sometimes works as Truth's assistant on the road, because Truth knows that he can trust him. His name is Anthony and he's really nice and smart. He's a sophomore, and he's going to school for civil engineering."

I guess you really can't judge a person by their family. What if someone judged me because of Dreya? Yuck.

"Okay, so Truth has a nice cousin. That is possible," I say. "I would just be careful kicking it at any of Truth's events."

"It's tripped out that you have only negative stuff to say about Truth, because according to Anthony, Truth has nothing but great things to say about you."

I lift my eyebrows in surprise. "I'm shocked that he has anything to say about me at all."

My cell phone buzzes. It's my mom calling. "Hello, Mommy," I say.

"Sunday! You need to get home, right now."

My heart rate quickens. "Is there something wrong?"

"No, honey, nothing wrong at all. I just got home from work and you have some mail from Epsilon Records today. It looks like a check."

"Did you open it?"

"No. Do you want me to?"

"Of course!"

I get up and walk away from my friends, because I don't want them to see the expression on my face when my mother reads me the dollar amount.

I hear her rip the envelope open, then I hear her scream, and then she drops the phone.

Finally, she picks the phone up, and says, "Thank you, Jesus! Thank you, Jesus!"

"How much is it?"

"I have never seen this many numbers on a check. It says one million, six hundred, eighty-eight thousand, four hundred fifty-seven dollars, and twenty-three cents."

Next, I scream! Mystique told me that the check would be huge, but I had no idea that it would be that big.

"Mommy, that's almost two million dollars."

"Yes, it is. What do you want to do?"

"I have no idea."

"Well, let's not do anything yet. Let's pray, and then meet with a financial adviser tomorrow."

"That's a good idea. Okay, Mommy. You know you can give notice at the post office now. You don't have to work there anymore."

My mother laughs out loud. "Two million dollars of your money is not enough to cause me to quit my job. That's why people end up broke again after they get a windfall. You can help me out, but there's no way I'm quitting my job yet."

"But, Mommy . . ."

"No, I won't hear of it."

"Okay, Mom. Dreya's calling me on the other line. Maybe she got her check too."

"Go ahead and talk to her, and come over here tomorrow morning."

"Okay, bye." I click over to Dreya. "Hey. What's up?" She's crying. Oh no. Not a good sign.

"Did you get your check?" Dreya asks.

"Yes, I did. Did you get yours?"

"Yes," she bawls. "It was only for thirty-two thousand dollars! That ain't no money."

"Thirty-two thousand? That can't be right! Your album went gold."

"Big D said that I spent thousands of dollars against my advance on my apartment, clothes, and my car. He said that because I didn't write any of the songs, I only got about twenty-five cents on each sale."

"But . . . I mean, it's thirty-two thousand dollars you wouldn't have had before, Dreya. You should invest it. You're moving to New York with Evan, so you won't have any expenses, right? Just save your money."

"Big D said that you and Sam made more money off my record than I did, because y'all had songwriter and producer credits on my record and on yours."

So that's why my check is so large. I made money off of her sales and my sales. I want to feel sorry for her, but I can't because everyone told Dreya she was spending way too much money on everything.

"Well, maybe on your next record you should try to get some songwriter credit. Like you should take a stab at writing some of your own lyrics. That way when it's time to get paid, you're more than just an artist."

"Yeah, it's whatever. Everyone wants to treat the artist like crap, and there wouldn't be a project without the artist. I started this off for you, Sam, Big D, and everybody else. If it wasn't for me hooking up with Truth, none of y'all would have anything popping. But I'm the one looking like Boo Boo the Fool."

I don't know how to respond to Dreya's rant. Part of

what she says is true. Her dating Truth was the catalyst to this thing with Epsilon Records. But we've worked hard—much harder than she has. No one is going to keep thanking her for our success. I know I'm not, and I know Big D isn't either.

"Dreya, I don't know what to tell you. If you need anything, you know I got you. Just say the word."

She laughs out loud. It's a dry, hurt, and bitter laugh. "You got me? *You* got *me?* That's real funny, Sunday."

"Well, I don't know what you want me to say, Dreya. Do you want me to be sorry about the money I made?"

"I don't want anything from you, Sunday. You always find a way to come out on top and make me the underdog. But trust and believe my time is coming. All of y'all are gonna be coming to me for favors."

"All right then, Dreya. I have to study for an exam. I'ma have to holla at you later."

I disconnect the phone call, but I stand here in total shock. Dreya lives in some kind of fantasy world where the entire universe is out to see her fail. I only want her to succeed, but I can't convince her of that fact.

All I know is that after I see that financial adviser tomorrow, I'm taking my mom shopping for whatever she wants. And then maybe, just maybe, I'll get a little something for me.

I'm a millionaire!

19

———

"First, we're going to set you up with some very safe interest-bearing investments. We'll put a portion of your portfolio into some of the riskier and more volatile stocks."

My mother interrupts the financial planner. "No, sir. I don't want any of her money at risk. I'll just put it in a savings account at the Bank of America down the street, if you talking about putting her money at risk."

"No, ma'am, not at all. We would never risk anything higher than earnings that she makes on her more stable stocks. We will not ever put her base million dollars into that pool of risks. That money will be collecting interest as always."

"Why does any of it have to be at risk at all?" my mom asks.

I answer this one. "The riskier stocks have higher reward. They make the most money."

She gives me and the financial planner some serious side eye.

He continues, "We're going to set up a retirement account for you, Mom, as a tax shelter for some of Sunday's money."

"What does that mean? Tax shelter?"

"The more money Sunday has liquid, the higher her tax liability at the end of the year. Money in a retirement account is not taxable."

Big D sent us to his financial planner, the one that he trusts. Evan also called with a recommendation, but I just felt a whole lot better with Big D's person.

"I'm sorry I have so many questions," my mom says. "We've never had this kind of money before."

"It's fine, Ms. Tolliver. I will answer every question to your satisfaction. I want you and Sunday to feel like you made the right decision trusting us with your portfolio."

I understand a lot more than my mother does, but I don't let on. I don't mind her asking questions. I think ever since she lost my college fund, she's been guilty as what. Now, she's just trying to make sure that I'm never in a bad spot again.

"Are you planning on making any large purchases?" the financial planner asks.

"Yes, I want to take my mom on a huge shopping spree, and at the end of my freshman year at Spelman, I want to buy a condo."

"How huge of a shopping spree are you talking?" my mom asks.

"However much you want! We can spend a hundred thousand dollars if you want to."

My mom pops me in the back of the head. "What are you thinking?" she asks. "Do you want to end up like Dreya, trying to figure out how she's going to stretch that little bit of money? No shopping sprees for me. She can buy her condo when she's ready."

"Ma, you don't even want a new car?"

"Nope. My car rides just fine."

She's going overboard with this not-wanting-to-spend-money thing. We're millionaires, for goodness sakes.

"Mom . . ."

"Sunday, I'm done talking about it."

"Well, I'm going to buy my boyfriend a gift. And I'm going to write a check to Spelman to pay one of my friends' tuition for the semester."

"Gia needs help paying her school bill?" my mom asks.

"Not Gia. Piper. She can't find her mother to sign off on her financial aid, so they're going through a legal process to state that she's an independent student. It takes a minute, so she was going to have to sit out next semester."

My mother hugs me. "Sunday, that is incredibly generous. Did she ask you to do this?"

"No. She has no idea that I'm going to do it. It's a surprise."

"Well, it's a big one! She's going to be so happy."

While the financial planner explains how a mutual fund works to my mother, I send Sam a text. **Are you in ATL yet?**

He replies: **Yep. Flight just landed. Can't wait to see you. Let's go blow some money.**

LOL! My mother is tripping like she doesn't want me to shop.

Whatever. I'll meet you back at your dorm in two hours. Got a couple of stops to make.

I can't wait to see Sam. We haven't spent time together since the American Music Awards a couple of weeks ago. His check was just over a million dollars. He didn't get the additional artist portion added to his, because he's not an artist. He's already hooked his mom up with a new house and car. I think she moves in this weekend.

After the meeting with the financial planner, I take my mom to lunch at Pappadeaux's.

"This isn't too expensive is it, Mom? Or do we need to go to Denny's?"

She laughs. "Okay, Sunday, I get your point. I just don't want you to blow all this cash."

"Mom, when have I ever been that foolish? Have a little faith in me! Didn't you raise me to always handle my business?"

"Yes, I did."

As we walk into the restaurant, I hear the screams of teenage girls. "OMG! OMG! That's Sunday Tolliver! We love you, Sunday!"

I smile, and hope that they'll calm down before everyone around them starts to stare. "I love y'all too!"

After I sign a couple of autographs, we go into the restaurant and are seated almost immediately. That's one of the perks to being a celebrity, I suppose. I never have to wait for a table anymore.

Once we're seated, I open my iPad. Time to check the blogs for the daily gossip. Some artists don't do this, but they're not related to Dreya. I have to check to make sure my name is not in the news.

"Oh my goodness," I say when I read the headline.

"What is it?"

I can't even read it out loud because I've got my hand over my mouth. The headline says Zillionaire's Love Child Revealed.

With much hesitation, I click on the link. Inside there is a picture of a toddler that looks a whole lot like Zac, down to his big hazel eyes and dimples. Actually, the baby is a dead ringer for Zac.

The story says that the little boy is two years old. Zac and Mystique have been together for four years. Anyone can do the math. If this is Zac's baby, then he's been unfaithful to Mystique.

The waiter comes up to the table and asks, "Are you ready to order?"

My mom orders her favorite fried fish platter.

"And for you, miss?" the waiter asks me.

All of a sudden, my stomach is tumbling and the butterflies are dancing a jig. "Can you just bring me some water with lemon and that's all?"

"Aren't you hungry?" my mother asks.

When I think about the fallout of this little news tidbit, my stomach lurches. The biggest question hovering in my mind is who told Mediatakeout.com about this baby? Who was the source of this story? Only someone with insider scoop would dare leak this information.

Someone with insider scoop who hates Mystique's guts.

I hope that it's not Dreya, but something tells me she was behind it all.

Things are 'bout to get ill.

20

Mystique storms angrily through the living room of her Atlanta penthouse. She's rarely ever here since Zac's mansion is bigger and better than her spot. But today, the day after that blog post went out to the Internet world, she doesn't want to be anywhere near Zac.

She's invited me here, along with her mother. I'm not sure why my presence is needed, but I'll do what I can. I have no idea what advice to give in this situation.

"The baby looks just like Zac," Mystique says, pointing at the still-open blog post on her iPad.

Ms. Layla studies the picture closely, "Well, it looks a little bit like him, but really, this could be anyone's baby."

"What did Zac say about it?" I ask.

"When I asked him, he said he couldn't believe that I would think that a gossip blogger was telling the truth. Now, he won't take my calls."

Hmmm . . . that sounds really suspicious to me, but I

don't know if I should say this to Mystique. If it's not the truth why would he stop talking to her? Sounds like he's guilty to me.

"Where did the story come from?" I ask. "Knowing who started the rumor will help you get down to the truth of the matter."

"I already had my assistant email the bloggers. No one is giving up their source."

"Well, what does that mean?" Ms. Layla asks. "Don't they know how important you are? You are the biggest star in R & B."

"You only as big as your last hit," Mystique says.

"Okay . . . so if the baby is Zac's, then what? Are you going to leave him?" I ask.

"I don't know. Probably not."

Call me crazy, but if she's going to stay with Zac whether the baby is his or not, does it make any sense to have all this drama?

"So why not just let the story die down? People will forget after a while, and then it will go away. Don't address the rumors."

Mystique stops pacing and stands in front of me. "Do you think that I'm worried about Zac having a baby? That is the least of my worries."

"Well then what is the issue?" I ask.

"Most people love me. I don't have enemies. At least I didn't think I had enemies, but whoever put this information out is deliberately trying to hurt me."

Ms. Layla shakes her head. "Maybe Zac has an enemy. This makes him look bad, not you."

Mystique shakes her head back and forth in frustration. "No, Mother. No! Anyone who would have this secret and tell the bloggers is trying to destroy me and Zac's relationship. That's a *woman* thing to do, not a guy thing. This is a swipe at me."

"If it is Zac's baby, maybe it's the mother," I say. "Maybe Zac isn't taking care of his responsibility."

"Let me tell you something about Zac. If he has a child out there, then that child is living in the lap of luxury. He would never let a child of his go uncared for."

"Who would want to hurt you, Mystique?" I ask.

"Your cousin."

Now I've figured out why she's invited me here, although I had pretty much guessed it already. If she thinks I have any influence with Dreya, then she's going to come up short. Dreya does exactly what Dreya wants to do.

"I don't think Dreya is your enemy."

"She is. But, in the past she's been completely harmless. Now that she's living with Evan, she's a dangerous enemy. One who can hurt my career."

"So, what do you want me to do? Do you want me to talk to her?"

Mystique shakes her head again. "No, I don't want you to talk to her at all, or even deal with her. I don't want you to write any more songs for her record until we find out who is trying to destroy me."

I feel the frown come over my face. Is she asking me to not deal with my own family? Who does that? If Mystique thinks that she can control me like she controls everyone else around her, she's got another think coming.

"Epsilon Records hired me to do the songs on her

album, Mystique. I'm getting paid by them. And plus, when her record comes out, that's more money for me."

"Are you saying that you're not on my side?" Mystique asks. "If it wasn't for me you wouldn't have a career."

I laugh out loud. "Believe it or not, you sound a lot like Dreya right now. She takes responsibility for my career too. Everybody wants to have the credit for blowing me up."

I stand to leave, but Mystique rushes over to me and takes both of my hands in hers. "Sunday, I don't mean to sound crazy, but your cousin is after me. She wants to take my spot, and she doesn't have nearly enough talent to think that she can, so she's going to try to do it the dirty underhanded way."

"It is my goal to stay out of anything between you and my cousin. Don't make me choose between you and my blood. This is my family you're talking about."

"Humph! What good is family when they stab you in the back? Do you know that Dreya tried to get you dropped from Epsilon Records when I signed you to my label?"

"What?"

"Oh! You didn't know that! She asked Caterina and Lawrence to reconsider putting money behind you, because you didn't have a unique sound. She even threatened to walk away from her deal if they didn't drop you."

"I know she wouldn't walk away from a record deal. She's wanted this too badly."

"Of course she wouldn't, but Epsilon called her bluff. And then they told her that they would never be controlled by an artist. Why do you think her marketing and video budget was so low? Why do you think you became their darling all of a sudden?"

Wow! This is crazy. I thought that I became the Epsilon Records standout because I was the better, less drama-filled, artist. But it was only because they were *punishing* Dreya? I can't believe this.

"Dreya's done some things to me in the past, but no matter what she does, I am who I am. And I don't hurt my family. That's not how I roll."

"One day, Sunday, you're going to see that family isn't all it's cracked up to be."

Ms. Layla says, "Do you think Mystique doesn't have sisters, cousins, aunts, and uncles to bring into the industry? Dealing with family members makes you weak. They use your blood against you."

"You all don't know my family. Tollivers stick together. My family doesn't make me weak. They hold me up when I'm weak. I'm stronger because of them."

21

It's hard for me to look at Dreya across the table. I feel like this perfectly browned turkey is the only thing that's keeping me from jumping on her and slapping her upside her head. Aunt Charlie keeps looking from me to Dreya as if she's trying to figure out the reason for the tension.

"So, how much was your check, Sunday?" Aunt Charlie asks. "Dreya is barely making minimum wage, according to her check. Seems to me like they're pimping y'all."

My mother purposely didn't share the details of my royalty payment with Aunt Charlie. She knew that Aunt Charlie would spazz the heck out if she knew that I was a millionaire.

But right now, I don't care if my aunt gets angry. Dreya is coming at me like we don't have the same genes in our DNA.

"My check was almost two million dollars."

I hear my mother drop a pan in the kitchen. The clanking on the floor isn't loud enough to make Aunt Charlie close her mouth, which is hanging wide open.

"Did you say million?" Manny says. "My cousin is balling! Did I ever tell you that you are my favorite cousin, Sunday? And . . . did you know that I loooove Transformers? If you didn't buy my Christmas present yet, Optimus Prime is waiting for you at Toys R Us. He only costs like fifty dollars. But you've got a million, kajillion dollars so it's all good."

Everyone stares at Manny like he's crazy. My mother brings in a pan of her famous macaroni and cheese and then she sits at the table. Everything smells and looks so good. Dressing, greens, candied yams, mashed potatoes. Delicious.

So tell me why both Aunt Charlie and Dreya look like they're about to be sick.

"Is Sam coming?" my mother asks. "I thought you said he would be here."

"His mom is having a huge dinner. She's never been able to have her holiday dinner catered, but since he's a millionaire now too, she hired a lady at their church to make a feast for their entire family."

My mom scoffs at this. "Really? I enjoy cooking for my family. Hiring a caterer seems like a waste of money to me."

"I guess you can do that when you're a millionaire."

I know I'm being a stinker, but I'm furious about what Mystique told me. I talked to Big D, and he confirmed the story. He said that Dreya was feeling desperate after she saw the negative light she was painted in on the first reality show. She thought that she was going to end up without a record deal.

I understand feeling threatened, but it doesn't explain her playing me out. I would never do that to her.

Aunt Charlie says to Dreya, "If Sunday's check is over a million dollars, then you need to get with somebody at Epsilon about the rest of your money. They didn't calculate something correctly."

"Oh, it's correct," I say. "Dreya didn't write one song lyric on her album. Didn't they tell you the songwriters and producers make more money than the artist? She could've contributed to writing, but she really doesn't have that talent. Then, she spent most of her money on stupid stuff, like getting her own apartment, just so she could have Truth come and go as he pleased. That's why she's got a minimum-wage check."

Aunt Charlie's lips form a tight line. "You're enjoying this, aren't you?"

"Not at all. I don't have time to enjoy anyone else's sorrow. That's not how I roll, but it does prove something to me, though."

"What's that?" Aunt Charlie asks.

"That karma is real. What goes around comes around. When you do dirt, you have to pay for it."

My mother pinches my leg under the table. "Let's pray," she says. "This is Thanksgiving, the time to give thanks for blessings."

"Great and small," I add.

My mother leads the prayer, but no one seems to be paying any attention to her. Dreya doesn't even bow her

head, she just glares at me across the table. Aunt Charlie
has angry tears streaming down her face.

But we all say "Amen" when the prayer is done.

"I'm surprised that Dreya is here with us for dinner," I
say. "Doesn't Evan have some huge Thanksgiving ban-
quet planned? Weren't you invited?"

"I didn't want to go to his Thanksgiving dinner. I
wanted to have some of Auntie Shawn's turkey and
dressing," Dreya says through clenched teeth.

"Why would she have Thanksgiving dinner with him?
He's in New York City, and we're her family," my mother
says.

"Oh, I know we're her family," I say, "but she doesn't
really seem to care too much about family. Plus since
she's going to New York to live with him, wouldn't that
make Evan her family? Or do you have to get married for
that?"

My mother slams her fork down on the table. "Sunday, what is wrong with you? You've been nothing but
messy since you sat down at this table."

"I'm sorry, Mommy. It's hard not to be messy when
you're talking about Dreya."

"What are you tripping on?" Dreya asks. "Oh, I know.
You're mad about Mystique's little paternity issue. I
don't know why everybody's all twisted about that. I
think Mystique would make a good stepmother."

I burst into fake laughter. "You think I care about
Zac's random stray baby? I couldn't care less about
that."

"So what you tripping on, then?" Manny asks. " 'Cause

y'all ruining my dinner. Auntie, can I have some macaroni?"

"Yeah, what *are* you tripping on?" Dreya asks. "You
need to get your head out of Mystique's behind."

"Forget about Mystique for a minute," I say, "and ask
yourself what you've done to me. Think long and hard. If
you go back far enough you'll figure it out."

Aunt Charlie says, "Y'all need to stop all this bicker-
ing. You're cousins. Aren't you working on some new
music for Dreya? Let's focus on that. We're still about
getting this paper."

"I agree," my mother says. "Let's not bring up past
hurts. That's not what God would have us to do."

It's so funny how they're always trying to remind me
that Dreya is my cousin when it's time to help *her*. No
one ever tells Dreya to remember that I'm her cousin
when she's making my life horrible.

"I don't know if I feel like working on Dreya's record.
I don't feel inspired," I say.

"You write songs for that conniving Bethany, but not
your cousin?" Aunt Charlie asks. "You letting this little
check go to your head, I see."

"Ask Dreya what she did. Ask Dreya how she went to
the heads of Epsilon Records and asked them to cancel
my contract. Ask Dreya how she was so threatened by
me, that she tried to ruin my shot."

"What?" Aunt Charlie asks with a genuinely shocked
expression on her face. I'm glad she's surprised, because I
thought that she was in on Dreya's scheme. At least now
I know that I don't have to be angry at my aunt too.

"So now you know," Dreya says. "I knew you'd find out at some point."

"Yeah, I know. And that was beyond foul."

Dreya nods slowly as she chews a mouthful of food, and then swallows. "I was doing what I had to do."

"Dreya, you apologize to your cousin right now," Aunt Charlie says. "I didn't raise you to turn on your family."

Dreya cracks up laughing. "Really? You're only saying that because Sunday has a million bucks."

"Almost two million," Manny says.

"Right, little brother, almost two million. And Mommy is greedy. So, she's making sure she stays in good with her rich niece," Dreya says.

"You don't talk to me like that! I gave birth to your ungrateful tail," Aunt Charlie says.

"Tell your mother sorry," my mom says.

"Nah, Auntie Shawn. I'm not going to be able to do that, and I'm not apologizing to Sunday either."

"You're not going to sit at my table and disrespect your mother, Dreya."

Dreya stands up. "Then I'm out. Thanks for the grub, Auntie. I'll holla."

Everyone sits in silence as Dreya storms out of the house and slams the door. Aunt Charlie has tears in her eyes, but I can't tell if they're angry tears or sad tears.

I put a forkful of food in my mouth. Cornbread dressing is my absolute favorite food, but it doesn't taste good right now.

"I cannot believe her," my mother finally says. "I don't think I know that girl anymore."

"I know what's wrong with her," Manny says.

"What?" Aunt Charlie asks.

"She needs a whoopin'."

Manny's right. Dreya does need to be punished. She needs to know what it feels like not to have me in her corner.

22

"Sunday, are you okay? You look stressed the heck out," Dilly says as he turns some of the dials on Big D's sound board.

We're putting the finishing touches on Bethany's album, which is going to be released in the early spring. She's already laid down all of the main vocals and we're working on some backgrounds and ad-libs. Bethany is in the sound booth, so she can't hear my conversation with Dilly.

"*You* look stressed the heck out," I say. "You and Bethany kiss and make up?"

He nods. "Yeah, I guess. It felt like she didn't really give me a choice."

"Get the heck outta here. Everybody has a choice."

"She's in my face all the time. When I get out of school, her car is parked out front. When I show up at the studio she's already here, or she shows up if I get here first."

Not a good look for Bethany to be stalking a high school senior, even if he is as fly and as talented as Dilly. That's not cool at all.

Bethany speaks into the microphone. "How's my volume, baby?"

Dilly frowns and says, "It's cool."

"See what I mean? She's tripping." Dilly talks with his head to the floor so that Bethany can't read his lips.

"You want me to talk to her?"

"Only if it's gonna work. You sound like you're on a mission right now, though."

I am on a mission, I suppose. I've got a lot of pent-up anger left from the Dreya Thanksgiving fiasco yesterday, so yeah, a mission would be somewhat appropriate.

"Where's Sam?" I ask. "I thought he was gonna come in to finish this up with us."

"He is, I think," Dilly says.

As if I thought him up, Sam bounds down the basement stairs. He waves at Bethany in the sound booth and then opens the door to the lab.

I scrunch my nose up immediately. Sam stinks like marijuana, and it's not just on his clothes. When he kisses me hello, I can smell it on his breath, and see it in his glassy eyes.

"What's going on, bro?" Sam says to Dilly. "I got some beats for you. Radio-type joints for your record."

"That's what's up!" Dilly says happily.

When I don't join into the conversation, Sam looks back at me. I'm frowning with my arms crossed and hip stuck out to the side.

"What's wrong, baby?" Sam asks as he kisses my neck.

"Don't kiss me. You stink like weed."

Dilly says, "She's in the mood for a fight today, I think. I'd leave her alone."

"What's wrong, boo? You feeling hormonal or something?" Sam asks. He and Dilly burst into laughter as if there was some funny joke told.

There wasn't.

"Nothing is wrong with me, but something's wrong with you. When did you start using drugs, Sam? Seriously? You're about to be an episode of *Degrassi* on me? For real?"

Sam tries to hug me and I push him away. "Come on, Sunday. Weed is not drugs. You know that! It's just a mood enhancer. It's prescribed by doctors all the time."

"It's prescribed for people with chronic pain, and terminally ill patients. Last time I checked, you don't fall into either of those categories, or is there something you're not telling me."

Sam grins. "I am in chronic pain. I miss you so much when I'm in New York that my heart just hurts thinking about you."

"Cut the games, Sam. I don't like the weed. Point-blank, period."

Sam lets out a big sigh and shrugs. "Where are we on these ad-libs?"

"She's almost done," Dilly replies, "but I think she wants to have Sunday do backgrounds on a couple of songs."

"Okay. Sunday, you ready to get in the booth?"

I don't reply, I just walk out of the engineer room and

slam the door. Bethany smiles at me as she opens the door to the sound booth.

We hear Sam's voice over the speaker, "Okay, ladies. Let's do a few riffs on 'Visions of You.'"

This is one of my favorite tracks off of Bethany's album, although I do like most of them. Bethany's got a fun voice to write songs for. Her tones are deep and smooth and they wrap around the notes like shiny paper on a Christmas present.

"There are a couple of places on the bridge where you can harmonize," Bethany says.

"There are some places in the second verse too. Why don't you let me handle the vocal arrangement? I did write the song."

"Ex-cuuuuse me!" Bethany says. "It's not like I can't give my input. It is my project, isn't it?"

"Yep, but I know best when it comes to the music."

I hear the music come through the earphones. I find every place where a harmony would work and I put it in.

When the song is over, Bethany asks, "Is your voice going to be on all those parts?"

"No, I just recorded all of them, but Sam will only keep the best ones. Why? You got a problem with my voice being on your record?"

"Not really. Just don't want it to sound like a Sunday Tolliver single, you know?"

I nod. "I feel you."

"Do you think my record will do as good as yours did?"

I shake my head. "No. It'll do better. I'm probably

going to make more money on your project than I did on mine."

"Well, good. Because I'm probably going to need the money."

I let out a little chuckle. "Why? You owe some gangsters or something?"

"No, but I think I'm pregnant."

"Get the heck outta here! By who? Dilly?"

She nods and my mind reels. No wonder she's stalking him. She's carrying his child.

"Does he know?" I ask.

"No. I want to tell him, but he acts as if he doesn't care about me."

"He's in the twelfth grade, Bethany. Maybe that's why he doesn't know how to handle being in a relationship. I can't believe you hooked up with him. He's too young."

"Are you going to fuss at me, or are you going to help me find a solution?"

I don't know what to tell her. This totally sucks because her career is just starting and it's all about to be over for her, as soon as Epsilon finds out about the baby.

"You aren't going to tell anyone, are you, Sunday?" she asks.

"I want to tell Evan, but I won't. If he finds out, your record won't get released."

"I know, but it's a long time until the spring. It'll be hard to hide this."

"You won't be able to hide it."

"But I don't have to keep this baby, Sunday. I haven't decided yet."

I shake my head and drop the earphone.

"Are you kidding me, Bethany? Really?"

"Don't judge me, Sunday. I don't want a baby right now. Don't tell me you wouldn't be thinking about abortion if you were in my shoes."

I shake my head. "Nah, I wouldn't. But then again, I'm not trying to get in that position."

"Okay, Sunday. You're perfect. My bad."

I leave Bethany standing in the sound booth. It seems like everybody is going crazy. Sam is smoking weed, Bethany and Dilly are about to be parents, and Dreya has taken her hateration to new levels.

Is this what fame and fortune does to people?

"Sunday, are you okay?" Dilly asks as I sit next to the soundboard looking angry.

"No. I am not okay."

"I won't smoke weed anymore, Sunday, okay? I didn't know you'd get so twisted about it," Sam says.

"Who are you? You get up to New York City with Zac and you start smoking weed?"

For a brief second I think of Sam's club situation with the ecstasy. Could he have taken it willingly? Aarrgh! Now I'm doubting everyone and everything.

"This has nothing to do with Zac," Sam says. "I'm just living life."

"Okay," I say.

"So . . . Sam," Dilly says, "is it true?"

"Is what true?"

"Does Zac have a baby?"

Sam shrugs. "I have no idea. Me and Zac aren't really friends, so you know."

Not really friends? Hmmm . . . I'm not buying that.

They go to the club together, but they're not friends? And why is Dilly worried about who does and who doesn't have a baby? He needs to figure out his own paternal status!

"Dilly, what would you do if you had a baby out here? Would you help raise it or would you be out?"

Dilly's eyes widen. "I don't want a baby right now. My sister and brother would probably help me take care of it, but I'm not ready to be a dad."

His whole comment has me furious! I can't stand when boys get what they want, but when it's time to pay the piper (the figurative piper, not my homegirl Piper) they want to dip like they ain't have nothing to do with it.

"If you aren't ready to be a dad, then why you out here hooking up with no protection?"

Dilly shakes his head, and his face is bewildered. "Um . . . come again. What are you talking about? I . . . uh . . . always use protection."

"You didn't with Bethany."

"What? Is that crazy chick saying I got her pregnant? She's tripping! I didn't get her pregnant."

Bethany steps into the engineer area right as Dilly is throwing his tirade. "Do y'all need me for anything else, tonight?"

"Yeah," Dilly says. "I need you to stop telling people that I got you pregnant."

"Sunday!" Bethany cries.

I shrug nonchalantly. "It just came out. My bad."

"Your bad? Wow. That's the last time I tell you anything in confidence."

"If you are pregnant," Dilly says, "that baby isn't mine. No way it could be mine."

Bethany bursts into tears. "Dilly, I don't know why you're being so mean to me now. Just a few months ago, you were really feeling me."

"You want to put this out there in front of Sunday and Sam? All right, then. I stopped liking you because you and your whole family are ghetto. And even though you got a record deal, you're still a groupie at heart. I saw you all over Zac once at the studio, like a stray cat that somebody gave some milk."

OUCH! Dilly just nuked Bethany. I mean totally obliterated her. Her face is the color of a candied apple you get at the carnival.

Sam says, "Look, man, you ain't got to disrespect her all like that. That ain't cool."

Dilly points in Bethany's direction. "Then tell this crazy chick to stop telling people she's pregnant by me!"

"You know what? I don't even care about what you say. You're gonna be looking stupid when I get that paternity test," Bethany yells. Then, she storms out of the lab and up the stairs. We can hear her heavy footfalls (stomps) on each step.

"Look what you started!" Sam says to me.

"I didn't start a baby between Bethany and Dilly. They're the ones who did."

"No, but you sure did start this evening's drama episode," Dilly says. "Thank you."

They are probably right. No . . . they *are* correct. I did start this mess tonight. I feel like everyone's negativity is getting to me—becoming a part of me. And the real Sunday Tolliver is the most positive person you'd ever want to meet. Is this industry going to destroy who I really am? Or is this music business bringing out a side of me that I never knew existed?

Maybe I just need to get away. Or perhaps I need to go to one of my mother's "prayers of the righteous" all-night prayer vigils, because I sure could use a few miracles right now.

23

"Can we go out to the club?" I ask Gia as she reads a novel on her bed. "I so need to go out tonight."

I need to seriously unwind this weekend, and I do not feel like kicking it with the Reign Records crew—at all. Too much tension and stress with them right now. Dreya and Mystique looking for ways to destroy one another, Sam turning into that stereotypical producer who takes ecstasy at clubs and smokes weed, Bethany is pregnant—maybe by Dilly—and Zac has a love child!

All of this is too much activity for me.

"Hope told me there's a party bus tonight making stops at all the campuses. We just have to call this number to make a reservation and we pay when we get on."

"That's what's up," I say.

"We're not getting trashed, right?"

"Oh, no! Of course not. I just like the idea of not having to drive."

"Cool, then I'm going to text Piper and Meagan."

"Must you?"

Gia laughs out loud as she pulls out her phone. "Of course. They are our crew. And Piper's feelings would be so hurt if we went on the party bus without her."

"Oh, all right! Text her then! But they better not be on any drama tonight!"

After Gia makes our party bus reservation, we pick out our looks. Gia selects a long-sleeved purple mini-dress that she rocks like a blouse over a pair of skinny jeans. She piles a huge amount of chunky beaded necklaces that give her a bohemian hottie effect.

I decide on skinny jeans too, but I pair a fitted blouse and some boots with mine. I quickly flatiron my hair and pin it up on one side.

"Makeup or no?" Gia asks.

"I'm not wearing any. Is Ricky coming?"

"I don't know. I didn't tell him I was going. I was thinking this is a night to kick it with my girls."

"That's what's up!"

Luckily, Spelman is the first stop for the party bus, so we get to pick our seat. We settle in the middle, in case the back gets too rowdy and the front is too lame.

Piper says, "I'm glad we're going out tonight! I have something to celebrate."

"What are you celebrating?" Gia asks.

"My tuition is paid in full through the rest of the school year. There was a private beneficiary."

"Really?" I ask. "Why do you think they picked you?"

"I have no idea, but I'm not gonna look a gift horse in the mouth."

"Is it a loan?" Meagan asks. "Do you have to pay it back?"

"No, it's a gift. Like a scholarship."

"My mother would call that a blessing," Gia says. "Don't try to figure it out, just enjoy it."

While I talk to Piper, I can't help but zoom in on the piercing in Piper's nose.

"Did you *really* pierce your nose?" I ask. "What would make you do that?"

Piper touches her jewelry self-consciously. "Naw, girl. This is a magnet."

"Oh! Then it's cute!"

The bus stops in front of the residence halls at Georgia State and a gang of students, mostly girls, get on the bus. They nearly fill the bus. Hope squeezes in the seat with me and Gia.

"I'm so glad y'all came!" Hope says. "I was gonna kick it with my girls from the dorm, but none of them wanted to go."

Gia says, "Sunday needs to hang out and de-stress."

"Don't we all?" Meagan asks. "She doesn't hold a monopoly on stress."

We all give Meagan a crazy side-eye look. I think Meagan is the type of chick who's used to being the queen bee of the group. I'm not sure how she feels about me getting so much attention. The ironic thing is that I don't even *want* people to treat me special.

Meagan appraises Hope's outfit—looks her up and down as if she's an editor at *Vogue* creating a best-and-worst-dressed list. "You look fabulous, girl," she finally says.

"Thank you! But I feel like I underdressed! Look at Gia. She's ready to walk a runway."

"You know how I do!" Gia says, and then bursts into a flurry of giggles at her own stuntin'.

Piper turns around in her seat and frowns. "What's wrong?" Gia asks. "Why you got that stank look on your face?"

"There's this chick in the back of the bus, mean mugging Sunday."

I groan and shake my head. So not in the mood for haters tonight. Or Dreya fans. I sure hope that Piper is mistaken.

"Maybe she's looking at someone else," Meagan says.

"Ignore it," Hope says. "She's probably some jealous girl."

"Do you think you need a bodyguard?" Gia asks. "Mystique has one, right?"

"Ugh! No!" I say. "I'm nowhere near as famous as Mystique. I hope I never need a bodyguard."

"Look, we're here at the first stop. Club Kaleidoscope."

"I've never been here," I say as I take in the psychedelic colors on the sign above the door. "I hope it's jumpin'."

There's a line in front of the club that wraps around the corner. I look down at my high-heeled boots and frown.

"Oh, man! Look at this line!" Piper says, expressing exactly what I'm thinking.

Meagan says, "Why don't we use this whole American Music Award–winning, number-one-on-the-*Billboard*-chart status to our benefit?"

"What are you suggesting?" I ask.

Meagan's eyes gleam. "I'm suggesting that we walk right up to the front door and strut in like VIPs."

"What if they don't recognize me? I'm gonna look stupid as what!"

This is a valid concern, because so many people in Atlanta are "celebrities." They either starred in a reality show or *worked* with Tyler Perry (the word *worked* being debatable). If I don't get recognized at the door, and it goes to the blogs, then I would be so embarrassed.

Piper says, "You've had two reality shows on BET and your video is in heavy rotation on a regular. Trust, the club's management has been waiting for you to show up. They know you go to Spelman."

I take one final glance at my cute boots, feel my big toe pinch, and say, "Let's do this!"

There are butterflies river dancing in my tummy as we stride confidently to the front of the line. I'm hoping, hoping, hoping that I don't end up with egg on my face because that will be sooooo embarrassing.

I can hear people in line whisper, "Is that Sunday Tolliver?"

As we get close to the front of the line, someone yells out, "Hey, Sunday! Love you, girl!"

I turn to the girl, smile, and wave. "Hey! Love you back!"

When we get to the front of the line, I don't even have to say anything! The bouncer gives me a big smile. Then he pulls out VIP wristbands and gives them to all of us.

"What's the cover charge?" I ask as I pull out my ID.

"For you and your girls, no cover. But we would really

appreciate if you could leak a few pics of your fun night here at Kaleidoscope."

Meagan yelps as soon as we're inside. "See! I told you! You are a celebrity, girl! Get used to the special treatment!"

"Does that mean we're her entourage?" Hope asks.

Piper nods and says, "Yep! And we are a *hot* entourage."

"Yes, we are," Gia says. "We need our own reality show."

On our way to VIP, we see Ricky and DeShawn standing close to the dance floor. Gia lifts an eyebrow, giving her face an irritated look. I guess she didn't know Ricky was going to be here tonight.

DeShawn walks up and gives me a hug. "Hey, pretty! Y'all looking real fly tonight."

"Come with us to VIP!" Piper says.

Okay, nobody told her to invite DeShawn to the VIP section, but I guess we can't invite Ricky without inviting DeShawn. Did I mention that when DeShawn hugged me I got a whiff of his cologne and it is off the chain! He smells like he took a bath in it, but it is really nice.

"Will they let us in?" Ricky asks.

"Do you know who she is?" Gia asks. "This is Sunday Tolliver, right here! Superstar!"

We all burst into laughter and make our way to the VIP section that is really just a curtained-off section guarded by another bouncer.

The bouncer raises a hand to Ricky and DeShawn. "Where are your wristbands?"

"They're with me," I say. "They just weren't at the door with me."

He nods and waves them in. Phew! I thought my star power had run out for a minute. I guess I'm still a celebrity!

We all sit around two large tables—well, all of us except Gia and Ricky. They heard a song that they like and didn't make it past the dance floor.

DeShawn says, "This is what's up! I don't think I've ever been in a VIP section of a club."

"Me either," Piper says. "But I gotta say, I thought it would be a little livelier."

Meagan laughs, "We're the party! Soon, they'll start letting people in here, just so they can say they partied with Sunday Tolliver."

Weird! People are going to brag that they hung out behind a curtain with me? Well, I guess if I'm going to be the party, I better get my partay on!

"Come dance with me, DeShawn," I say.

A gigantic smile forms on his lips. "I thought you'd never ask."

DeShawn and I get on the dance floor just as Mystique's new dance track starts to play. It makes me think about Mystique's drama with Zac. I wonder if it's true that he has a baby. And if he does have a child, does that mean he thinks it's okay to be unfaithful to your girlfriend with a groupie? And if he feels that way, do I really trust Sam when he's with him?

"What are you thinking about?" DeShawn asks. "Because you sure aren't here with me right now."

"Oh, I'm sorry. I have a lot going on."

"Well, loosen up and have a good time. Isn't that why you came to the club tonight?"

I nod and smile at him. I can't help it; his smile is infectious. And he's not flirting with me anymore, which I totally appreciate. I think he's either biding his time until I'm not with Sam anymore or he's moved onto the next hottie.

"I came here to forget about the drama."

He tips my chin upward with his index finger and grins. "Then forget about it."

I take his advice and start getting into the music. I'm nowhere near as good a dancer as my friends, but I try to get into my groove.

Meagan was right. After a couple of songs, the VIP section starts jumping. They've let in quite a few people and the dance floor is filling up. We dance hard for about five songs in a row, but then I'm thirsty. Plus, the next song is a slow song and I'm not trying to go there with De-Shawn, especially now that he's acting like a gentleman.

"DeShawn, I need a break," I say breathlessly.

"I wore you out, huh?"

"Pretty much. I'm gonna sit down for a minute."

"I'll walk you back to the table."

When we get back to the table, Meagan is sitting alone, but she doesn't look lonely. She's got a Coke and a plate of wings keeping her company. Hope and Piper have found partners and they're tearing it up on the dance floor.

"Meagan, you want to dance?" DeShawan asks. "I've still got some energy."

Meagan shakes her head and takes a sip of her Coke. "No thanks. I cannot get all hot and sweaty; I just might meet my Morehouse man here tonight. I shouldn't even be eating these wings without a breath mint or some gum. Sunday, do you have some gum?"

"I have a mint."

"Good enough."

I hand her a mint and then I make myself comfortable in the booth. The soft, cushiony leather is perfect. It's like it molds to your behind or something when you sit down. I don't think I'm moving from here for the rest of the night.

"DeShawn, I think I'm out for the count," I say. "You might have to snag Piper or Hope."

"Aw, man! Okay, Sunday. If you feel like dancing again, come and get me."

My feet are straight throbbing in these tiny boots, so I know I won't be going to find him anytime soon.

"The party bus will be back in an hour so we can go to the next club," Meagan says.

"Oh, y'all aren't staying?" DeShawn asks.

"Nope," I reply. "We're going to . . . where are we going, Meagan?"

"Club Pyramids."

I roll my eyes. I should've known they were going to pick Club Pyramids. It's one of the hottest clubs in the A that allow minors to come in.

"You don't like Club Pyramids?" Meagan asks. "It's a really fly spot."

"It's owned by Dilly's brother, Bryce. We don't have really great history. Actually, he's somebody I try to avoid at all costs."

"Would it make you more comfortable if Ricky and I came with y'all?" DeShawn asks.

"You don't have to do that, DeShawn. . . ."

"It's cool. I want to."

The way he says this . . . takes me back to the uncomfortable place with him. He says these things that taken by themselves, as just words, are totally non-flirtatious. But while he speaks, he gazes into my eyes with a look of concern on his face—as if he's my boyfriend.

I just don't know what to do about him.

"Okay, then. I think Gia wants Ricky with her anyway so that will work out great."

"So, don't leave for your party bus without telling us, okay?"

I nod and DeShawn takes his swag back to the dance floor, to whip it out on some unsuspecting girl, who will just melt in his hands from the power of his suave-i-tay. Not!

"You and DeShawn looked really good out there," Meagan says. "Almost like a boyfriend and girlfriend."

"Don't start. I'm dating Sam."

"I think you should have a college *friend* at least."

"I've got lots of friends."

Meagan laughs out loud. "Okay, I mean a friend that is a hot boy. That kind of friend."

"Why would I do that when I have a boyfriend?"

"You have a missing-in-action boyfriend," Meagan says. When she sees my look of irritation, she backs down. "Okay, sorry. You have a wonderful boyfriend."

Sam being wonderful is definitely debatable now, but I won't have Meagan doubting his loyalty.

"Look, there are those girls from the bus," Meagan says changing the subject away from Sam. "They're across the room at the table close to the VIP curtain."

"What girls? Do I know them?"

"No," Meagan says. "It's the girls that were looking at you with so much attitude."

Oh, those girls. I didn't really get a good look at them on the bus, so I turn slowly to my left so I can identify them if I have to later. There are three of them, and there's one in the center wearing a gold dress and a long curly wig. She looks like a Mystique knockoff. Kind of like one of those purses you buy in New York on Canal Street. Perfect until you give it a close inspection. Even from the corner of my eye I can tell the chick is glaring at me.

"She's still giving me shade too," I say. "I don't even know her, so I don't know what her problem could possibly be."

Meagan laughs. "It's called hating, I believe, in your street vocabulary. Perhaps even hateration."

"What do you mean in my *street* vocabulary?"

"Don't get twisted. You know what I mean."

"I think I know what you mean. Why don't you tell me what hating is called in your high-class, high-paid, cottage-in-the-Hamptons-owning lingo."

"Where I come from we call it envy, plain and simple."

Envy. An amped-up form of jealousy.

I turn to the girl and look at her face-to-face. Her face twists into a frown. A frown that wasn't there before.

Envious sounds like the precise nickname for her.

24

Club Pyramids is exactly how I remember it. Loud music, obnoxious neon lights flashing everywhere. Okay . . . it's ghetto. There. I said it. But they are at least attempting to be an elite club. Now, they're trying to take in some of that concert money and are booking artists for shows.

We use my celebrity status again to get to the VIP area without waiting in line or paying anything extra. This special treatment is something I could definitely get used to. Without question.

This time in the VIP, I see some very familiar faces. Some I want to know that I'm at the club—others I'd rather not deal with. Bad-boy rapper Truth is there with his entourage. I'm actually surprised he'd show up here since Bryce has got ties to Zac, and since Zac beat the tar out of him for hurting Dreya.

I roll my eyes at him as I walk past with *my* entourage. Okay, my entourage is soooo lame compared to the crew of gangsta-looking, wife-beater-wearing thugs with Truth. And the girls . . . well, let me just say that I'm sure at least one of them has either a gold-digging or a baby-mama-to-the-stars career ahead of her.

"It could be worse," Gia whispers to me as we pick out our own table in the corner. "Your cousin could be here too."

Dreya has been keeping a pretty low profile since the story about Zac's love child broke. That's why I think, even more, that she had something to do with that leak. I haven't heard a peep out of her since Thanksgiving. Maybe she's not talking to me because she's still angry about my millionaire status.

We all slide into a long booth that has miniature tables in front of it. From our seat we can see the door to the VIP area, which is good, because I'm checking for those jealous chicks from Georgia State University. I have to make sure I watch my back.

I hear Bethany's first single blast through the speakers. I don't tell anyone that I wrote the song or that it's even Bethany. I want to see my friends' reaction to the song without any biases or input from me. The song is called "Stop the Presses" and it's about a girl who finds out that her boyfriend broke up with her on Facebook. It was inspired by a letter from one of my fans.

Piper is the first to speak up. "Ooh, I really like this song. Does anyone know who that is? She's got this little gravelly thing happening with her voice! It sounds really good!"

"I wasn't really paying attention until the second verse," Gia says. "She came in blowing on that part."

"Yeah, she did," Ricky says. "But why are girls always singing about some dude doing them wrong? Like y'all don't do guys wrong sometimes."

"Sure, girls do dirt too," I say, "but we typically don't get caught!"

Hope jumps up and gives me a high five. "I know, right! Guys can be pretty clueless to when they're getting played."

"Like tonight," Gia says, "I will assume that no chicanery was taking place with you and DeShawn kicking it to the club, even though you didn't tell me you were going clubbing."

Meagan says, "Okay, that has nothing to do with what we're talking about."

"Yes, it does," Gia says. "I was about to say that if you were up to something, you probably would realize that you couldn't really creep this close to campus, because it would always get back to me. That's how I know you *aren't* up to anything."

Ricky shakes his head. "Okay, y'all, she's been looking for an opportunity to fuss at me since she walked up into Kaleidoscope and saw me in there with DeShawn. Ain't nobody trying to creep, Gia."

"Okay, well, I was just wondering why you didn't mention your little boys' outing when I told you I was going on the party bus with my girls."

"Because DeShawn invited me at the last minute."

DeShawn bursts into laughter. "Man, don't put me in

this! Next time, I'll remind you to check in with your girl first. I don't want you to get grounded. Then we might not get to hang at all."

"Thank you," Gia says.

Ricky scrunches his face into a frown. "What! I don't have to answer to Gia. I'm a grown man. Now . . . out of courtesy, I will *try* to remember to tell you where I'm going."

"Out of courtesy?" Gia asks.

"Yep. That's what I said."

Gia nods with her entire body. It's a mad, kinda filled-with-attitude nod. "Okay. I see you, Ricky. Mr. Georgia State football."

Gia is dead serious, but Ricky cracks up laughing. He even holds his side as his giggles come fast and furiously.

"What is so funny?" I ask. " 'Cause my girl look like she fixing to open a can of whoopin' on you."

"She looks just like her mother. I wish you could see yourself, Gia. You look just like Gwen when she's about to tell somebody off."

This melts Gia's anger completely, and while she doesn't join the laughter, she does smile. "Whatever, boy. You get on my nerves."

"There are those girls again," Piper says. "They stay stuntin' in VIP like they're somebody. Wait, are they someone we should know? Do they sing?"

"I don't know. Maybe," I say. That would explain the mean-mug faces they keep throwing over here.

This time they walk straight up to our table. The ring leader says, "Are you still kicking it with Sam?"

"Although you clearly know who I am," I say, "I have no idea who you are. I only share my personal business with friends."

She laughs out loud. "I'm Porche and my best friend's name is Rielle."

Okay, so now this makes sense. Rielle is the girl Sam asked to prom after he and I had our first break-up-to-make-up session. I don't know the girl, probably wouldn't recognize her if she came in the club too, because I only saw her a couple of times on the prom pictures.

I shake my head. "Now I know your name, but you're still a stranger. Sorry. Would you like an autograph?"

Snickers around the table from my friends. Well, laughter for Piper. Everyone else tries to be slick with theirs. Piper has zero finesse. I should say she scores a negative ten on finesse. We're gonna have to school her on that.

"Naw . . . I don't want your autograph. I'm far from a groupie."

"Well, then what is it that you want?"

"To let you know how your man comes to visit my girl on campus at Georgia Tech every time he's in town. And how she lost her virginity to him on prom night. Your boy's a dog. I just thought you should know."

I open my mouth to reply, but nothing comes out. Porche and her two sidekicks crack up laughing. "I see you not talking sideways now are you, pop star? You know what else? Sam bought Rielle a new computer when he got his check from Epsilon Records. It's a nice laptop. He must still be getting some, because I don't know a guy who would do that if he wasn't reaping some benefits."

Gia and Hope both jump up at the same time. Gia says, "Y'all can cluck on. It's funny y'all have heard all about Sunday, but she don't know anything about you chickens."

"Sounds like your friend is a sideline ho," Hope adds.

A million thoughts are running through my mind. Like the first lie that Sam told me. He said Rielle was nobody. Not a girlfriend, just someone he asked to prom at the last minute. And then he said they only kissed. Now this chick is saying they hooked up. Then, I wonder if we can make it through this.

I don't know how to feel about this. I'm just used to Sam being kind of corny and not the type of dude who would be a player. But I never knew Sam at his own school, and in his own element. I only knew him from the studio. I have no idea what Sam was like before I met him.

I feel like I don't know him at all.

Porche and her girls wait a few seconds longer as if they're waiting for a response from me. I can't and won't give them one. The only person I want to talk to is Sam.

Finally, when they realize there's not going to be a fight or any drinks thrown (because I'm much too classy for that), the three haters actually leave the VIP area. I guess they were waiting for the perfect time to lay this on me. I'm glad they leave the VIP, because I don't know how long I can hold it together, and I definitely don't want them to see me twisted.

"You okay, Sunday?" Piper asks.

I shake my head. "Of course I'm not okay."

"Don't get too upset yet," DeShawn says. "They could be lying."

That's true. They could be. But how would they know that Sam got a check from Epsilon Records? Like, that's too much information for them to have if they weren't in communication with Sam at all.

"Yeah, I would get the whole story first," Ricky says. "You can't just believe their side. That's not fair to Sam."

The worst part is, Sam is not in town right now. He's in New York City doing who knows what with who knows who. I can't even talk to him face-to-face, and this is definitely not a phone conversation.

I send Sam a text. **Can you get a flight out tomorrow?**

He texts back. **Is everything ok?**

No, I reply.

What's going on?

Need 2 c u. Will talk when you're here.

Sam doesn't reply for a few moments to the last one. I wonder why. Is he going through a laundry list of dirt in his mind? Is he trying to backtrack? Trying to figure out what could've gotten back to me?

Finally, he says, **I'll be on the first flight out. Will call when I land.**

Tomorrow, then, I'll know for sure. I'll look into Sam's face and ask the tough questions, and I think I'll know if he's lying. Hopefully, the truth will be written all over his face.

And then . . . well, I don't know what will happen

next. But at the end of the conversation, I'm either going to have a boyfriend, or I'm going to be single and free to mingle.

Didn't I say I was going out tonight to get away from the drama? Well, it looks like I can't escape it. The foolishness is following me.

25

A heavy sigh escapes me as I see Sam lingering outside the dorm in his jean jacket with fur trim and boots. He's got on sunglasses and a hunting cap, even though it's not really sunny at all. The hunting cap looks warm though.

Sam smiles brightly when he sees me. He runs up, scoops me into his arms, and kisses my neck. "I missed you, girl."

"I missed you too, Sam."

"What's wrong, Sunday? Why does your voice sound like that?"

"Like what?"

"Like you're ready to rip my head off about something. I haven't even been to the club with Zac since that other thing went down, so I hope you're not still tripping on that."

"Can we take this conversation outside? Let's take a

walk. I don't want everyone in the dorm knowing my business."

"It's like that?" Sam asks. Now he sounds worried, and I don't do anything to calm his fears. He should be worried.

Once we're outside, and a safe distance away from the dorm, Sam says, "Okay, Sunday, what's going on? I don't want to have to guess, either. Can you just come right out and tell me?"

I give a hoarse chuckle. Seriously, he thinks he's calling the shots here? Really? He should be going over all the dirt he's done in his mind and answering his own questions. He knows what's up.

"Okay, I won't keep you in suspense, because I don't play games. Rielle's best friend Porche came up to me at the club. . . ."

Sam rolls his eyes and sighs. "I can't stand Porche."

"Well, she didn't say anything about the two of you being friends. She did say that you and Rielle are still pretty tight."

"Let me explain. . . ."

With those words, I feel my stomach drop. He's not supposed to say, *Let me explain.* He's supposed to say that Porche is a raving lunatic, and that everything that comes out of her mouth is a lie. He's not supposed to have an explanation.

"Explain what? Explain how Rielle lost her virginity to you on prom night? You told me that you two only kissed. How does one lose their virginity by kissing?"

Sam sighs again. "Okay, so I didn't tell the truth about that. I did hook up with Rielle on prom night, but it was just that. A hook-up. We weren't dating, and you and I were about to get back together. I didn't want to mess that up."

"You thought telling the truth was going to mess up what we had? Wow. This is crazy. How many other things have you lied about, Sam? Did you lie about the groupie in New York? Was she even a groupie? Were you drugged, or was that all your idea? Do you see the issue I have here, Sam? Tell one whopper of a lie, and then I have a hard time trusting you at all."

I'm pacing back and forth now, making a shoe-print trail in the frosted grass outside my dorm.

"I already answered your questions about that, Sunday, and I'm not going to go back over that again."

"Now you're telling me what you *not* going to do? That's really funny. I just have another question, though, since you admit that you lied about hooking up with Rielle. Why did you buy her a laptop? Is she still your hook-up buddy? Or maybe I'm wrong. Maybe she's the main girlfriend and I'm the side piece. She was first, right? And since we haven't hooked up yet, and I currently have no plans to go there with you, maybe she's the top chick."

Sam shakes his head. "Her mom goes to church with my mom, that's how the whole prom thing happened in the first place. My mother always liked her. And . . . well . . . when we hooked up, Rielle told her mom, who told my mom. They're acting like I owe her something because they think I broke her heart."

"Did you break her heart? Did she think you guys were more than just hook-up buddies?"

"I don't know. . . . Maybe. But when I got my check, my mom mentioned that Rielle didn't have a laptop and that her mom had mentioned it at church. My mom thought buying it for her would be a good way to apologize."

This whole story sounds crazy. First he lies about hooking up and then he tells me some preposterous story about doing a good deed?

"Are you still messing with her?"

"I don't think I should have to answer that."

I stop pacing and am now face-to-face with him. "You don't *have* to do anything."

"No, I'm not still messing with her. Come on. We're about to go to her campus right now. She'll tell you."

I cock my head to one side trying to figure out Sam's plan. It could be a move of desperation, or maybe he already had the heads-up from Rielle and they put their heads together. I mean, if I was Rielle, and my boyfriend was making millions dealing with a hot pop/R & B artist I might want him to keep making money. If I dump Sam, I don't know if he'll still be considered a member of the Reign Records family.

"I'm not going anywhere with you. I've got all the information I need to make a decision."

"You're gonna go off the word of that skank Porche? She's just mad because she tried to hook up with me and I turned her down."

He's quite the ladies' man these days, I see. I could believe that Porche would do that, but it doesn't change anything about the lies that Sam has already told.

"I was going to give you this when I saw you next. I didn't want it to be like this . . . but . . ."

Sam hands me a little jewelry box.

"What is this?"

"Open it."

I open the box and there's a pretty diamond ring inside.

"It's not an engagement ring, or anything like that. It was meant to be a promise ring."

Before I can stop myself, I laugh out loud. This is the least perfect time for him to give me a promise ring. Promise of what? That he'll stop telling me lies and hurting me?

"What exactly are you promising, Sam? I'm a little bit confused, I think."

"I know I've messed up. Big-time. But everything I hid from you, everything I didn't say is only because I wanted so much to be with you. I know you, Sunday. Everything is all or nothing. I knew if I told you about hooking up with Rielle, you would've never forgiven me, even though we were on a break at the time."

"We were on a break?"

"Well, I can't even say it was a break. You'd placed me in the friend zone and wouldn't let me out, and you were flirting with Truth."

"I am not about to rehash all that. Bottom line, you lied to me. You are not about to turn this around and make it seem like this is a me thing."

I place his ring box right back in his hand.

"So you're not going to accept my ring."

"I'm not. I'm a millionaire. If I want diamonds, I'll buy my own."

I quickly walk away, leaving Sam standing outside. I

don't want him to see the angry and sad tears streaming down my face. He cannot see me crying. It's not even fair that I am.

Pop-star status might get me VIP access in the club, but it sure doesn't do a dang thing for my love life. I feel the opposite of VIP. I'm like the busted chick who got to the door of the club and got turned away for looking too basic.

How am I going to get over this?

26

All day, after Sam's visit, I stay in bed crying. I don't know if I'm angrier than I am sad, but I just know the tears won't stop coming. I've already used two boxes of tissue and I'm working on a third.

Gia and Hope come back from church and they've got food. I can smell it.

"We've got a bunch of good stuff," Gia says.

"Comfort food," Hope adds.

Gia nods as she pulls out paper plates and forks. "When you're sad you have to eat. Good food helps release mood-enhancing endorphins into your bloodstream. It's like taking a Prozac."

"She means that it'll make you feel better. Piper and Meagan are on their way with chocolate, ice cream, and movies."

"Movies? What kind of movies?" I know they better

not bring a romantic comedy up in here. I will hurl that thing across the room if they do.

"I was against it, but they're bringing scary movies," Gia says. "I'm not a fan, but it's better than nothing, I suppose."

A few scary movies are perfect. Maybe I'll be too petri-fied to even think about Sam's deceptive ways.

My phone buzzes, and I don't even check it, because Sam has been texting me and calling me nonstop. He keeps saying that he cares so much about me, and that Rielle is nobody. In my opinion, you don't buy *nobody* a laptop. Seems to me that a nobody wouldn't get any gifts. A nobody wouldn't even have your number.

Maybe if it was just them hooking up for prom night . . . maybe I could've understood. But, it wasn't just that. He's *still* dealing with her. How could he still be dealing with her when he's supposed to be with me? Aren't I enough?

"When are they going to get here with the movies?" I ask.

"Meagan just texted me and said they'd be here in five minutes," Gia says.

Hope hands me a plate of food full of my favorites. Fried chicken, mashed potatoes and gravy, collard greens, can-died yams, and macaroni and cheese. Of course, it's from the Busy Bee Café.

Sam and I loved to go to Busy Bee.

"What do you want to drink?" Gia asks. "We've got Pepsi, sweet tea, and apple juice."

"Sweet tea."

"I should've known. You're a native."

This makes me laugh, because it is so true. Sweet tea is like water to me. We probably drank more tea than any other beverage in my house growing up.

Sam loves my sweet tea.

I take a huge bite of food and try to push the thoughts of Sam out of my mind. This macaroni and cheese is so good. I don't know what Gia meant when she talked about endorphins, but if it means good enough to slap yo' mama, then I agree.

"It's good, isn't it?" Hope asks. "This is how my mother cooks."

Gia laughs out loud. "Your mom is not this good a cook."

"I know you're not talking. Your mother's pancakes taste like shoes. And not even fly shoes. They taste like Payless shoes."

"Okay, I'll give you that. My mother cannot cook."

I crack up at the back-and-forth cousin banter. If they're purposely doing this to distract me, then it's working, because they are too funny.

There's a knock on the door, and it's Meagan and Piper. They've got huge grocery bags and movies.

"Okay, so it's going to be an *Aliens* marathon. We've got *Alien*, *Aliens* and *Aliens III* and *Alien vs. Predator*. Then, we also got *Takers*."

"What does that have to do with the alien theme?" Gia asks.

"Absolutely nothing. But it's a movie full of hotties," Piper says. "Hotties are good, right?"

We all burst into laughter. My phone rings, and this

time it's Mystique. I know her ring tone. This one I will answer.

"Where have you been?" Mystique asks instead of saying hello.

"Here, in my dorm. What's up?"

"I've been texting you all day, and you hadn't replied. It was like you fell off the face of the earth or something."

I roll my eyes at her dramatics. I'm about five seconds away from saying something crazy. Not in the mood for anyone being theatrical today. No one except me. If I want to throw a tantrum I will.

"What's going on?" I ask. "What's so important?"

"Do you know about this thing with Bethany supposedly being pregnant?"

Big sigh. Not caring about Bethany's foolishness right now. But of course, Mystique doesn't know what's going on with me. If she did, she'd be more sympathetic. I think.

"Yeah, I know about it."

"So when were you going to tell me? Evan is going to freak out! She's got a record coming out in the spring. She can't have a baby."

I shrug. Not my issue. "What do you want me to do about it?"

"Convince her not to have it!"

"I can't do that. Plus, I can't even think about that right now."

"Why not? What's the matter with you?"

"Nothing. What's up with Zac's love child?"

Groan from Mystique. "Well, we're at least talking now, but he still won't give me an answer one way or the other. I'm pretty sure it's his kid by the way he's been acting."

"Wow. Well, keep me in the loop on that."

"I will if you answer your phone."

"Call me. Don't text me." I can't take the chance of seeing one of Sam's begging text messages.

"Okay. Evan is calling a Reign Records meeting for later this week. It's going to be at Zac's house."

"Is Dreya going to be there?"

"Yeah, I think so. I heard she finally got settled in at Evan's house. She had the master suite redecorated."

That makes me sad. Dreya is too young to move in with a man, but neither she nor Evan see anything wrong with it because she's legal. My aunt Charlie didn't try too hard to stop her either. I think if it had been some broke dude with no cash, that no one could've stopped Aunt Charlie from regulating. But because Evan is worth three hundred million dollars, he gets a pass.

"Dreya is an idiot," I say. "I hope she gets what she wants."

"She wants to be the biggest star in the world. Evan will try to make that happen."

"At whose expense?"

"Anyone who gets in his way, I guess."

"Well, let me get off the phone with you. My friends are here, and we're about to watch movies. Catch you later."

"Don't forget to talk to Bethany."

"Whatever."

I disconnect the call and take another bite of food. "What are we watching first? *Aliens* or hotties?"

Gia plucks a movie out of Piper's hand. "Let's save the hotties for last."

"Are y'all ready for final exams?" Hope asks. "My dad is going to freak out if I don't get good grades."

"I'm ready. I don't think I'm going to have a problem on any of mine," Gia says.

Piper says, "I just can't believe the semester went by this fast. I mean, it seems like we just got here and now we're about to be done with the first semester."

"I'm not worried about exams either," I say, "but I do have to study. I'm not one of those people who can cram for tests. I've been hitting the books whenever I can, but I'm not sure it's enough."

"How do you even find time to study? It seems like you're always at the studio or at the club or somewhere," Meagan says. "I admire you, though, because I couldn't do it with all those distractions."

There's another knock on our door. I have no idea who that could be since we're all here.

Piper opens the door. It's DeShawn. He's got a greasy-looking bag in his hand.

"Oh, I see y'all already have food. I was just bringing Sunday some pizza from my favorite pizza shop."

"DeShawn! That's so sweet," I say. "Give it to me! If I gain ten pounds by the end of next week who cares! I don't have a boyfriend anyway!"

"Aw, don't say that," DeShawn says. "You and old boy are gonna work it out. He'd be stupid not to beg your forgiveness."

DeShawn brings the pizza over and gives me a hug. He feels strong and his cologne is incredible. But I'm so not thinking about how hot DeShawn is right now. I'm thinking that I have to stay completely away from him, because all boys are the same. Players. All they need is a groupie and the opportunity.

"Thanks for the pizza, DeShawn. I appreciate it," I say.

"Okay. Call me if you need anything."

I nod and smile. I have no intention of calling him, but there's no need for me to hurt his feelings since he's being so nice to me.

When DeShawn leaves, all of my friends burst into laughter. "What's so funny?" I ask.

"Nothing except the fact that DeShawn is so pitiful," Gia says. "He's been digging you ever since that video shoot y'all did."

"I know. He's nice, but I'm not about to get with anyone else anytime soon. Sam messed it up for all the boys on all the campuses."

Meagan shakes her head. "My grandmother says, 'one monkey don't stop no show.' You need to just dust yourself off and get back in the saddle."

Piper raises her hand. Gia says, "Yes, Piper."

"Excuse me, I'm having a really hard time believing that anyone in Meagan's family said that. There was a double negative somewhere in that sentence."

This makes everyone crack up, including Meagan, who is not really all that cool with jokes about her family.

"Don't hate on us because we're bougie," Meagan says.

"Turn on the movie!" Hope says. "I'm ready to see Sigourney Weaver kick some alien booty."

Even though there's that ever-present pain in the pit of my stomach whenever my mind wanders back to Sam, the laughter is helping. A lot. My mother always says that laughter is good for the soul. I guess it's also a good remedy for a broken heart.

27

"*Teen Cosmo* wants to have you on the cover of their magazine next month." Evan catches me by surprise with this, because we're not anywhere close to talking about photo shoots.

We're at Big D's studio working on some music for Dilly's album. Well, me, Dilly, and Big D are working on music. Sam was instructed to leave some pre-recorded tracks, so that I don't have to see him. I'm only doing the hooks for the songs, because Dilly writes his own lyrics. He's a true emcee.

"Why do they want me? I'm not a model or anything like that."

Evan laughs out loud. "Oh, sweetie, by the time we get done with you, you're going to be a model, actress, singer, songwriter, and all of the above. We're just getting started."

"Okay . . ."

"But for this cover, they want you because you are in college and in the music industry. They're doing an issue on the best colleges for fabulous girls."

"Sounds hot. When is the photo shoot?"

"In a week or so. They're going to do it at a studio in downtown Atlanta. They'll have several different backdrops and all of them something scholastic."

I wonder if Dreya's heard about this. She's probably going to throw a hissy fit, and talk about all of the opportunities that Reign Records is making for me and not for her.

"Cool, just let me know where to be."

Dilly comes downstairs with a bag of chips and a few cans of soda. He hands me one, pops one open for himself, and sets the rest of his snacks down on the table.

"Did you hear from Bethany?" Dilly asks.

I shake my head. "Hear from her about what?"

"She said she had a miscarriage. But I don't think she was ever pregnant. Not by me anyway."

This is an interesting development. If Bethany was pregnant, I think she may have gotten an abortion. Mystique was pretty adamant about pushing that decision on her. Mystique probably told her that if she had the baby her career would be over, which was probably the truth.

"She didn't seem like she was lying when she told me. And think about it. She never wanted you to know. If she was lying, why would she want me to keep a secret?" I ask.

"Maybe she knew you wouldn't keep it. I don't know. I'm just glad that it's over. If I never see her again, it'll be too soon."

Evan says, "No such luck, young homie. You're going

to be doing some shows with her. That duet you did on her record is hot, and it's going to be her first video."

Dilly sighs. "Oh my God. This is a nightmare. I can't stand her."

"Listen," Evan says, "you keep that inside these walls. When you get interviewed, you let everyone know that it's all love at Reign Records. I don't care what beef y'all have with each other. Keep it in the family."

I wonder if that goes for Mystique too. She's definitely got beef with Zac right now, and possibly has some with Dreya.

"Are you going to marry my cousin?" I ask.

Evan cracks up. "Nah. It definitely isn't like that. She is having the time of her life in New York, and spending lots of cash. She would like to be the first lady of Reign Records, but she needs a little bit more polish."

When he says *first lady,* does he mean his girlfriend or something? And does the use of *first* mean that there are seconds, thirds, and fourths? See a smart chick asks these things, and a silly girl just takes the American Express Black Card and calls it a day.

What am I saying? At least she's getting gifts out of it all. I let Sam play me for free.

"I thought Mystique was the first lady of Reign Records," Dilly says. "She's the biggest artist on the label."

"The first lady is whoever I say it is," Evan says. "Trust and believe, Drama is going to be even bigger than Mystique. She's been floundering around with absolutely no guidance. No offense to Big D. He doesn't really know what to do with a diamond in the rough like Drama."

Diamond in the rough? That's new. And not the way I would describe Dreya at all. Well, definitely the rough part, but not the diamond part.

"Bethany has potential to blow up too," I say. "Her voice is incredible, and she really blossoms as a solo artist. I think she always hid behind doing background vocals when she sang with me and Dreya. She never wanted to sing a lead."

Evan nods. "She is good, but she's too silly. She's going to do something to mess it up if she isn't careful. She's the type of artist that gets dropped from a label and no one understands why because they were so talented."

"Since you have so much commentary on everyone," I say, "what do you think about me? Am I going to crash and burn?"

"Sunday, you could have it all. You are a legend in the making. But you know what? I don't think you really want it. I can't understand why you're still doing this college thing. You're already a millionaire. All you need is a street degree. You could get one of them hanging with me."

"I love music, but all this invasion of privacy . . . I don't know if I want it. I feel like there are people out to get me. Every time I go out to a club, I'm wondering who's going to say something sideways to me."

"Yeah, that's all part of it. First things first though, you probably need to drop out of Spelman. I haven't been pressuring you, but the more popular you get, the harder it's going to be. You have to watch everyone. You won't know who's trying to be your friend just because of your money."

"None of my friends have asked me for anything. . . ."

"Yet. They haven't asked you for anything yet. Just give them a minute."

I shake my head and frown. "You don't have any faith in people, do you?"

"Nah. Everyone lets you down at least once. Set your expectations there and you won't get hurt."

This makes me think of Sam. I had high expectations of him. I thought he was going to be a faithful boyfriend even though he was living in New York City. He's let me down twice and it's not even December yet.

"Dilly, I've got finals next week so I won't be in the studio. Feel free to get anything done that you need Sam for, because I won't be here."

"You two haven't squashed that yet?" Evan asks.

"Uh, no, we haven't and we're not going to squash it. And no, I don't recall asking you for your opinion about it."

"Okay, okay! I won't try to get you back with your boyfriend. But I do have an issue with you not being able to work with your main producer. You two have come up with some really good music. I don't want to see that disappear," Evan says.

I don't say it to Evan, but I think my days of making beautiful music with Sam are over. I can't see it ever being the same. Why did he have to go and ruin it all?

"Was what he did so unforgivable?" Evan asks. "Don't

act like you've never, ever lied in your life to keep from hurting someone's feelings."

"That's the thing. He didn't lie to keep from hurting my feelings; he lied so that I'd take him back. Unacceptable reason."

"I'm just saying, don't feel like it takes anything away from you if you forgive him and move on."

What is up with Evan the guru today? I'm so over his advice. First of all, I didn't ask for it. Second of all, it doesn't make any sense. Plus, his advice is self-serving anyway. He wants me and Sam back together, so that we can keep making him money.

"I'll think about it," I say, even though I have no intention of doing so. I just want Evan to leave me alone.

My phone buzzes with a text message. I almost don't look, because I'm not trying to read any of Sam's apologies.

But I do look and it's from Dreya. **Go on MTO right now.**

I pull up the celebrity gossip site on my phone. The headline reads: *MTO EXCLUSIVE! ZILLIONAIRE IS THE FATHER, MYSTIQUE LEAVES REIGN RECORDS AND WEDDING BELLS FOR MYSTIQUE AND ZILLIONAIRE.*

Before I can even tell them what the blog post says, Evan's phone starts blowing up. Usually, Media Take Out only posts once a day, but this story is too good for all that. They had to post it immediately.

"She did what?" Evan screams into the phone. "She can't decide to leave Reign Records. I don't care what Lawrence and Caterina said. I'm the brains behind all this. They don't know what . . ."

Evan stops midsentence when he notices that Dilly and I are staring at him.

"I'll call you back."

He disconnects the phone and says, "We have a meeting tomorrow evening at Zac's house. Mystique is no longer with Reign, but still with Epsilon. We have to figure out what to do next. Eight o'clock, tomorrow."

Evan storms out of the lab and leaves Dilly and I to make up our own answers.

Mystique's move is an interesting one. Evan thought he was holding all the cards and she just played the one she was hiding under her shoe. Epsilon Records needs Mystique's record sales, and apparently Zac has decided that he needs her too. Enough to put a ring on it.

This is just starting to get interesting.

28

Everyone's here, in Zac's conference room, and the tension in this room is so thick that you could spread it on a piece of toast and put jelly on top.

I'm sitting to the left of Mystique at the big table. Only because no one else wanted to take the seat. Zac is to the right of Mystique and at the head of the table. Evan is directly opposite him at the other end. Of course, Dreya is at his side. She keeps taking his hand in hers and stroking it. It is a surprisingly gentle gesture from her. Big D and Sam are in the middle seats, so I guess they're not pledging allegiance to anyone. Dilly and Bethany don't even get a seat at the table, so they just stand.

"Why'd you do it, Mystique? What are you trying to do to us? Reign Records was poised to take over the industry, and then you jump ship."

"Reign Records wasn't my idea. It was yours. I'm not

interested in commingling with a bunch of new artists. I've already paid my dues. No disrespect."

Evan sucks his teeth slowly and obnoxiously. "So you agree with her, Zac?"

"Yeah, I do. This is her career. I don't make decisions for her. If she feels this is the best move for her, then I won't argue."

Bethany asks, "Why is it such a big deal? We're all under Epsilon Records, right?"

"Because Evan wants to control me, and no one does that. I've been there already at the beginning of my career. I manage myself. I run my own business. Sorry, Evan. Nothing personal."

Sam keeps trying to make eye contact with me, but I look away every time his eyes try to meet mine. It's already hard enough with him in the room; I can't have him staring me down.

"I don't think we need her. She's a straight hater anyway," Dreya says. "She's hated on my cousin since the very first time she heard her sing. That's why she put her on Mystical Sounds. She just wanted to make sure that Sunday didn't get any bigger than she is."

Mystique's mouth opens and she looks at me. "Is that what you think, Sunday?"

"What? No! That's all Dreya. I did not approve that statement."

Mystique smiles sarcastically at Dreya. "You are just jealous, Drama. You've always wanted me to take you under my wing, like I've done Sunday. But the truth is, you're just too basic. And I know it was you who started that story about Zac's baby."

"What if I did?" Dreya asks.

"I'll have to thank you some time. The whole thing got us talking about family and marriage. I'll make sure you're invited to the wedding."

"A team of wild horses couldn't drag me there," Dreya says.

"Not so fast, Drama," Evan says. "Of course we'll be there. This will be the wedding of the year, and just the event for me to debut you as my woman."

Dreya squeals. "That's what's up!"

"Okay, I don't think any of this concerns me. I am just a producer," Sam says. "I just want to make music."

"It concerns you, because it concerns me, and it concerns Sunday," Big D says. "If Mystique is not the anchor of Reign Records, then who is going to be?"

"Drama will anchor the label," Evan says. "I just need a few months to clean up her image."

"I think it should be Sunday," Big D says.

"You've always thought it should be Sunday," Dreya says. "So that doesn't surprise me."

Evan says, "Ask Sunday how she feels about it."

"Why does it have to be about anchors, and who's on top? Why can't we just make incredible music and let the listeners decide?"

Evan waves his hand in the air as if he's proved his point. But then, I guess he has. "Like I said, Drama will anchor the label."

"Well, now I just feel like an uninvited guest," Mystique says. "I don't need to hear any Reign Records business. But please be our guest to continue your meeting in our home."

Evan jumps up from the table and storms out of the room with Dreya at his heels.

"Is that all? Can we leave now?" I ask, because everyone is looking all nervous and uncomfortable.

Big D says, "I don't want y'all to worry. We don't need someone to put us out there. We're going to let our music speak for itself. Bethany, your record is coming out next, and it's going to be incredible."

"Thanks, Big D," Bethany says.

"Then you, Dilly. Next year this time, we're going to wonder how we even worried about it."

Big D keeps talking about worrying, but he's the only one who sounds nervous. Reign Records, Epsilon, or whoever, as long as my tuition is paid.

Speaking of tuition, I've got some exams to prepare for. Plus, the sight of Sam is literally turning my stomach.

"I've got to get back to school. It's exam week, next week," I say. "We done here?"

"Yeah," Big D says.

"Let me walk you out," Sam says.

"I'd rather you didn't."

"Sunday . . ."

I shake my head and sigh. "Okay, whatever. Walk me out, then."

Once we're outside of Zac's house, Sam says, "Big D is going to come apart at the seams, you know that, right? He needs us. He thinks he's ready for Zac and Evan, but he's really just trying to look out for all of us."

"Big D will be all right. I'm sure his check was bigger than mine, so he got paid."

"What about us? Will we be all right?"

"Oh, I'm straight."

"So it's done, huh? We're done?"

I nod. "Yeah. I think so. But Evan wants us to still work together."

"Can you still work with me?"

Long pause from me. "I think I can, but I'm not sure."

"So . . . I'll give you a break from seeing me and then, when it's time to compose the songs for your next record . . . we can try."

I need to get away from him . . . immediately. His pitiful routine is not making me feel anything remotely close to pity. Actually, it's making me want to go straight upside his head.

Yeah, I can't look at him without feeling anger, or remembering his lies. Totally not ready to collaborate with him, and I don't know if I ever will be.

"I'm outta here, Sam. Take care."

Those words sound so much more final than I mean them to sound, but I think Sam gets the message. It's good-bye . . . for now.

29

Woo-hoo! I just finished my last final in English Composition. And I know I aced it even though it was purposely hard. My professor was evil.

One semester down, seven to go until I have my undergraduate degree. Then, onto law school. But one victory at a time. First, pass my fall-semester exams.

As I cross the courtyard on my way back to my dorm, Piper runs to catch up with me. She's panting and breathing heavily when she finally catches up to me.

"If you're breathing that hard from just running across the campus, you need to work out."

"I know, Sunday," Piper says between breaths. "I know it was you."

"You know what was me?"

"I know you paid my tuition."

I poke my lips out and roll my eyes. "I don't know what you're talking about."

"Whatever, Sunday. I see you don't want to admit it, but I'm going to thank you anyway."

I couldn't wipe the smile off my face if I tried. "I still don't know what you're talking about, but if I did, I'd probably say you're welcome."

Piper links arms with me and we walk back to the dorm in silence.

When we get to our room, Meagan and Gia are there, and they've got boxes of pizza and Pepsi—our favorite pig-out foods.

"It took y'all long enough to get back!" Gia says.

"Yes, it did!" Meagan says. "Now it's time to celebrate."

"What are we celebrating?" I ask.

Gia says, "We survived our first semester of being free-thinking women."

"Right," Meagan says. "Our first semester of taking the world by storm."

"Our first semester of being away from home," Piper adds.

"Our first semester," I say, "of sisterhood."

We toast with glasses of Pepsi and tear into the greasy, cheesy, and chewy, gooey pizza. If anyone had a question about why I stay in school when I've already made my first million, they could find their answer here. I haven't got it all figured out yet, but I'm getting there, and my friends are helping me learn.

I'm here to learn how to make a difference in the world. And I am here to find out who I am. With every new dilemma, I feel the old Sunday slipping away like a pair of knee-highs on my legs in the middle of summer-time.

And this is who I am. I am a student. I am a daughter. I am a (ridiculously talented) singer.

And I am a sister.

ON THE FLIP SIDE

Nikki Carter

ABOUT THIS GUIDE

The following questions are intended to
enhance your group's reading of
ON THE FLIP SIDE.

Discussion Questions

1. Is Sam's story about what happened at the New York City club believable? Did you believe him?

2. What do you think about Dreya and a rap career? Does she have what it takes to be a hip-hop diva, or should she stick to the pop star game?

3. Is there a future for Bethany and Dilly? Should Dilly kick Bethany to the curb, or should they have a full-fledged teenage love affair? Why or why not?

4. What's up with Mystique? Is she really down for Sunday or is she a secret hater?

5. What do you think of Sunday's new sister-friends at Spelman? Does Gia seem like a good roommate? What about Meagan and Piper? Do you see drama in the future for these two?

6. Who's going to snag Kevin? Piper or Meagan?

7. Seems like Sunday's friends are sorority crazy! Do you think Piper is Gamma Phi Gamma material? Should she even pledge, or is it a train wreck in the making?

8. Sunday. Sam. The breakup. Should they get back together or should Sunday walk away—this time for good?

Don't miss Nikki Carter's

Time to Shine,

available now wherever books are sold!

"Sunday Tolliver! Are you on your way to Mystique and Zillionaire's wedding?"

The paparazzi catches me off guard by jumping from behind a building as I exit my parked car in front of Mt. Pleasant Baptist Church in downtown Atlanta. Really? This bird is hiding at four o'clock in the morning trying to get the scoop? I mean, who is checking for Mystique wedding details at four in the morning? And anyway this is not the location for Mystique's wedding. It's actually one of the decoy spots. I will be picked up by another car to take me to the final location.

"I'm on my way into this church," I say.

The annoyed almost-reporter cocks her head to one side and sucks her teeth. She looks like she doesn't know whether or not to believe me. I certainly don't look like I'm going to a wedding. I'm wearing sweatpants and my hair is in a loose bun on the top of my head. But there is a full wardrobe and makeup crew at the real venue, so I don't have to worry about looking glam right now.

"You're one of her bridesmaids, aren't you?" the reporter girl asks.

I lean in closely and whisper, "I'll never tell."

The frustrated reporter rolls her eyes again and storms off, perhaps looking for someone more willing to spill their guts about the so-called wedding of the year. I won't share the details because, as a pop star myself, I don't like my business in the streets (or on the Internet) either.

I stride away from the irritated blogger chick. She can be camped out here for the next few hours and she won't be any closer to the truth than she is now. The plan is for each member of the wedding party to be picked up by shuttle bus at four-thirty in the morning. Then we will be taken to the top-secret wedding location. The wedding party doesn't even know where it is.

I can't believe Mystique was able to pull off something this complex when she and Zac (Zillionaire) only decided to get married a few weeks ago. News of Zac's love child hit the blogs and the next thing you know those two are heading straight to the chapel to get married.

When she asked me to be the one and only bridesmaid, I was kind of shocked. It's not like we're really close or anything like that. She gave me my first record deal and basically introduced me to the world as her protégée, but something has happened in these past few months. All of a sudden she got competitive, and did a few things that could be confused as hateration.

I duck into the church and hand my car keys to a security guy standing at the door. He will be in charge of dri-

ving my car from the church to another parking area—
not where the wedding will be held, but another fake location to throw off the paparazzi. Yeah, it's super cloak
and dagger up in this piece.

Then I see him.

The new ex-boyfriend of mine. Sam.

Ugh.

Like can I ask a side-bar question? Why do boys have
to lie all the time? Sam told me that he didn't hook up
with Rielle on prom night, and that was a big, fat, gigantic lie. He says he only lied because he didn't think I'd be
his girlfriend if I knew, and he's probably right. I
would've soooo kept it moving. But now, I really like (almost kind of love) Sam and he's hurt me.

Maybe I would've believed that he was all done with
Rielle after prom, but apparently he's still dealing with
her. He even bought her a laptop! Do I care that he did it
because she's poor and her grandmother heard that he
got a million-plus-dollar check? Um, no. We do not do
good deeds for side pieces.

And why is he smiling at me? Ugh. I can't stand him.

He's Zac's best man, for some ridiculous reason. They
aren't even friends. At all. Sam is his employee. Zac and
Mystique are probably trying to orchestrate a reunion or
some stupidity like that. But I don't care. Not trying to
hear that.

Sam crosses the church sanctuary to where I'm standing
in the back. He's still smiling like an idiot. I roll my eyes.

"So, they're sending a car for us," he says. "It should
be here soon."

I give him a tight nod and start playing with my iPhone.

I make a huge production out of putting my earbuds in, so he can tell that I'm listening to my music.

I wish my girls Gia, Piper, and Meagan were here with me. They didn't rank high enough on the celebrity list to get an invite to Mystique's wedding. They're not celebrities at all—they're my friends from Spelman College. Gia is my roommate.

Mystique told me that I could invite one of them as my guest since I don't have a date, but I decided against it. The two I didn't invite would inevitably be mad at me, and I'm anti-drama right now.

So I invited DeShawn. He's a hottie who goes to Georgia State and plays on the football team with Gia's boyfriend Ricky. He also models and was in one of my music videos. He's cool, he's a friend, and he flirts with me. It doesn't matter that I am not in the boyfriend-type mood. Having DeShawn with me at the wedding will, at least, keep Sam out of my face. I hope.

The wedding guests have to park their cars at a different location, and then they'll be driven to the top-secret wedding location. Mystique has sold exclusive rights to her wedding photos to *People* magazine, so it's like imperative that nobody take any pictures—paparazzi or guests. They're even hijacking people's cell phones at the door.

It's that serious.

After a few minutes, I hear another car pull up outside the church. Sam and I are given dark jackets and baseball caps to put on, as we exit the back of the building. We look like some ghetto spies.

Once we're in the car, I notice that the driver is one of

Zac's security guys. He drives us through Atlanta to a beautiful castle on Peachtree called Rhodes Hall.

"I can't believe they're getting married here. Right in the middle of everything!" I exclaim to no one in particular.

Sam replies, "This is the perfect location. No one would even suspect that they were getting married this close to downtown Atlanta."

I narrow my eyes in Sam's direction. I was not talking to him. Okay . . . so I know there are only two other people in the car besides me, and since I don't know the driver, it's pretty logical for Sam to assume that I'm talking to him.

But, since he also knows that I can't stand his guts right now, he shouldn't assume anything.

We're dropped off at the back gate of the castle, but since it's still dark outside no one can see us. Amazingly, there are no paparazzi hiding here. Maybe, it's because we took a roundabout way to get here. The church where we got picked up from is like ten minutes from the actual venue, but it took us forty minutes to get here.

When Sam and I walk into the building . . . wait. I do not like "Sam and I" put together in one sentence. That is so . . . ugh!

When I walk into the building (we don't care what Sam is doing), I see Mystique barking out orders like the bridezilla from the pits of Hades.

"Mother, please tell me that my veil is here. The custom-made diamond-encrusted veil that cost three million dollars to produce is here, right? Because if it's not here, someone's head is gonna roll."

Ms. Layla, Mystique's mom, puts a hand on her

daughter's back. It's a calming move, but it doesn't seem like it works.

"Honey, the veil is here. I just unpacked it. It is with Zac's security team now. Try to stay calm. You don't want to look frazzled in your wedding photos."

"Okay, Mother . . . I'm trying. I'm really trying. Where's Sunday? Is she here yet?"

"Present and accounted for," I say from the back of the room.

Mystique flies back to greet me and embraces me with a bear hug. Who is this? I'm afraid I have not met this emotional and affectionate person masquerading as Mystique.

"Sunday, I'm so glad you're here. I can't have anything else going wrong."

"I'm here too," Sam says.

Mystique smiles at Sam and then says to me, "Sunday . . . can you please, please be nice to Sam today? I want you smiling in my pictures."

I reply through clenched teeth. "I'll try."

Mystique seems to accept my reply. I'm glad because it's the best I can do. She rushes off to fuss at the florist, who apparently has brought an incorrect flower.

"Does this look like a calla lily?" Mystique asks in a high-pitched roar.

I take a seat and wait for someone to tell me what to do. I don't want to get in Mystique's path. Not today.

I know that if I ever get married (and that is so not in the plans any time soon), I don't want it to be like this.